Hiss Me Deadly

Chet Gecko Mysteries

And don't miss

Hiss Me Deadly

FROM THE TATTERED CASEBOOK OF

CHET GECKO
PRIVATE EYE

Bruce Hale

HARCOURT, INC.

Orlando • Austin • New York • San Diego • London

Requests for permission to make copies of any part of the work
should be submitted online at www.harcourt.com/contact
or mailed to the following address:
Permissions Department, Harcourt, Inc.,
6277 Sea Harbor Drive, Orlando, Florida 32887-6777.

www.HarcourtBooks.com

Library of Congress Cataloging-in-Publication Data
Hale, Bruce.
Hiss me deadly/Bruce Hale.
p.   cm.
Summary: Chet Gecko is hired by Principal Zero to
investigate the disappearance of valuable items from
Emerson Hicky Elementary—including Mama Gecko's pearls.
[1. Geckos—Fiction.   2. Animals—Fiction.   3. Schools—Fiction.
4. Stealing—Fiction.   5. Humorous stories.
6. Mystery and detective stories.]   I. Title.
PZ7.H1295Hi   2007
[Fic]—dc22   2007002952
ISBN 978-0-15-205482-3

Text set in Bembo
Display type set in Elroy
Designed by April Ward

First edition
A C E G H F D B

Printed in the United States of America

To my best buddy Betsu: Friends 4-eva, brah!

Hiss Me Deadly

A private message from the private eye . . .

I'm Chet Gecko, best lizard detective at Emerson Hicky Elementary. (True, there are no *other* lizard detectives, but let's not quibble over details.)

I am an only child. I have *only* one sister. And that's plenty more than enough, believe me.

I don't have to look up my family tree because I know that I'm the sap. When my sister got robbed, she turned to me for help. And like a dope, I jumped in with both feet.

But a simple case of theft soon grew more challenging than playing Chinese checkers on a bucking bronco. Valuables started vanishing from school, and the top brass called me in. True, I don't know all that much about theft, but I do know what time it is when a possum steals your refrigerator: time to get a new refrigerator.

I followed the twisty trail of clues until I'd unearthed more suspects than a zombie membership drive. The more I learned, the less I knew. (Of course, this happens to me at school all the time.)

The heat was on. As I drew closer to uncovering the shadowy puppet master behind it all, I got myself in a spot tighter than a blue whale's bikini. Would I make it out with my skin?

Not to worry. As any detective will tell you, it's always darkest before dawn. So if you're going to steal your neighbor's newspaper, that's the time to do it.

1

Sub Sandwich

You could attend Emerson Hicky Elementary for a long time without knowing its substitute teachers. And you could know its subs for a long time without meeting Barbara Dwyer.

And that would be just swell.

Barb Dwyer was a sourpuss porcupine with a face like a bucket of mud. From the tips of her many quills to the shapeless hat on her head, she was a surly sub, and she didn't care who knew it.

I could have gone my whole life without meeting her. But because Mr. Ratnose called in sick one gray Wednesday, we were stuck with the dame.

Through math and English classes she had ridden us hard, like a rhino going piggyback on a house cat.

We were taking a breather, doing some silent reading. Most of the kids favored *Winnie the Poobah,* our assignment.

I had slipped the latest *Amazing Mantis-Man* comic book inside old *Winnie.*

Private eyes like to live dangerously.

A gentle whisper broke my concentration.

"Chet?" It was Shirley Chameleon, leaning across the aisle.

I gave her a look. She was worth looking at. Shirley had big green peepers, a curly tail, and a laugh like the pitter-pat of raindrops on daisies.

Not that I cared about any of that. She was also a major cootie factory.

"Mm?" I said, glancing back at my comic book.

"Do you, um . . . are you going to the fair on Friday?" Shirley toyed with her scarf, one eye on me, one eye on the substitute teacher. (Literally. Chameleons have some gross habits.)

I leaned over. "Depends. Will they have clowns?"

"Why?" she said.

"Because I *hate* clowns."

"Who's whispering?" a voice snapped. Ms. Dwyer scanned the room.

We clammed up. A minute later, Shirley bent back across the aisle.

She batted her eyelashes. "I don't know about

clowns," she whispered, "but I do know that they're having a *dance*."

I knew it, too—the Hen's Choice Hoedown, where girls ask boys.

"I was trying to forget about that," I said.

Ms. Dwyer thundered, "No more whispering. Eyes on your books!"

Shirley gave it a rest for another minute. Then she murmured, "If you're, um, going to the fair, maybe you'd come to the dance with me? As my date?"

"Your *date*?!" I spluttered, shattering the quiet.

"That's it!" cried Ms. Dwyer. She waddled up the aisle toward me, quills bristling. "You! What's your name?"

Although I wanted to say *Seymour Butts,* I stuck with the truth. "Chet Gecko."

"You've disrupted my class enough for one morning."

I let my book drop. "But *she*—"

Ms. Dwyer noticed my *Amazing Mantis-Man.* "And you're reading this . . . this trash? A *comic book*?"

"It's research," I said. "For my science report."

"I don't care if it's *War and* frikkety *Peace*," she growled. The porcupine held her hand out for the comic. I gave it to her. "You, mister, will sit outside until you learn some manners."

Bo Newt chuckled. "Guess I'll see ya next year, Chet."

The substitute wheeled on my friend. "Would you like to join him?"

"Uh, no sir," said Bo.

"Ma'am!"

"No sir, ma'am," said the newt.

Ms. Dwyer gritted her teeth, then glared at me. "Well, what are you waiting for? Go and reflect on your bad behavior."

It's no use arguing with a walking pincushion. Followed by Shirley's mournful gaze, I rose and ambled out the door.

Five minutes of sitting on the hard cement was enough reflection for any gecko. My tuckus was going to sleep. But the sub let me stew.

On the far-off playground, little kids squealed with joy and freedom.

I sighed. Idly, I twirled the tip of my tail. No case to solve, no comic to read. It would be a long, boring timeout.

I couldn't have been more wrong.

Footsteps slapped down the hall. "Chet! Chet!"

The last thing I expected was my little sister. And yet, there she stood, big as life—Pinky Gecko, first grader and first-rate pain in the tushie.

"Little blister," I said. "What brings you here?"

She frowned. "My feet. But, but…how come you're sitting in the hall?"

"I'm on guard duty—watching out for cocka-poos."

"Cocka-whose?" she said.

"Never mind."

Pinky turned her woeful eyes on me. "Help me, big brother."

I pointed. "Okay, the loony bin is *that* way."

"Not funny," she said, pouting. "Mom's pearls, they're missing!"

I scratched my head. "Run that by me again?"

"The pearls." Pinky shuffled her feet. "I, um, borrowed 'em for show-and-tell."

"Smooth move, moth-brain," I said. "And what, you accidentally flushed them down the john?"

"I'm *not* a moth-brain," she said. "I showed 'em before recess. An', an' when I came back from recess, they…disdappeared from my desk!"

I stood. "Have you told your teacher, Miss uh…"

"Miss Flemm? I can't."

"Why not?" I asked.

Pinky's lip quivered. "She'll tell Mom."

"Yeah, so?"

"Mom doesn't know I borrowed 'em."

My eyebrows rose. "Ah."

"An', an', an'…" Her eyes misted up like dawn over Mosquito Lake.

Before the waterworks began, I gently placed my hands on her shoulders.

"And you want me to find the pearls, is that it?" She nodded. "Mm–hmm."

I chewed my lip. We'd had plenty of crime at Emerson Hicky Elementary—cheating, blackmail, vandalism, kids trying to take over the world. But no crook had made it this personal. No crook had *ever* picked on my family before.

My fists clenched. This punk was going down hard, like a skydiving brontosaurus. Why, I'd even tackle the case for free.

But I'd never let Pinky know that.

"You realize if I do this, you're gonna owe me big-time?" I said. "We're talking breakfast in bed, sharing desserts, no hassling me for two—no, *three* weeks..."

"A-anything you say." Pinky sniffed. "Just find the pearls."

I hate to see a reptile cry—even if she's my own flesh and blood.

"Stop your sobbing, sister," I said. "I'm on the case."

2

Bad Hare Day

After a long morning of pretending to learn stuff, a gecko needs to tuck into some serious grub. And I knew just where to find it—this funky little joint called the cafeteria. What it lacked in style, it made up for in quantity.

That Wednesday, Mrs. Bagoong and her staff had gone all eastern European on us. The menu boasted squash-bug blintzes, fruit-fly borscht, and a bunch of other stuff I couldn't even spell, much less identify.

I munched a heaping trayful while waiting for my partner and pal, Natalie Attired. She's an elegant mockingbird with a taste for puzzles and a wit like a razor's edge.

"Hey, Chet," her voice chirped from behind me. "What do you get when you eat onions and beans?"

"Ugh, don't tell me."

"Tear gas!" She cackled.

Make that a *dull* razor's edge.

Natalie settled in beside me at the table. "What's the word, private eye?"

"Kumquat," I said.

"Actually, I was hoping for two words: *new mystery*." She pecked at a fly in my soup.

"Hey! Keep your beak out of my borscht, and I'll tell you what's new." In short order, I laid out the case for her.

Natalie smoothed her feathers. "Your own sister, a client?"

"Yeah."

"The same sister you called *pure evil in a little pink dress*?"

"Well, yeah." I forked another bite of blintz into my trap.

"Either you're going soft, or we're getting paid a *lot*," said Natalie.

I chewed. "Listen, birdie. This goon picked on my sister. *Nobody* picks on Chet Gecko's little sister."

She cocked her head. "Except Chet Gecko."

I lifted a shoulder. "Well, of course. Anyway, I

get to write my own ticket with her. Pinky says she'll do *anything* to pay me back."

"And what big brother could resist that?" said Natalie. "Let's vamoose!"

Our first interviews should've been Pinky's teacher and fellow students. Unfortunately, they were all back in class.

Staggered lunch periods can make grown PIs weep with frustration.

But not us. We switched to Plan B: a trip to the custodian's office. You want to get in trouble? Ask the principal. You want the lowdown on the playground? Ask a janitor.

Maureen DeBree's cubbyhole was headquarters in the never-ending war on grime. Her assistants have come and gone. But Ms. DeBree remains—a mongoose without mercy—leading the cleanliness charge.

I rapped on her half-open door. "Ms. DeBree? It's Chet and Natalie. Do you have—?"

A rabbit's furry face peeked through the gap.

"You're not Ms. DeBree," said Natalie.

"And you're not Ham and Rye, the world-famous food jugglers," said the rabbit. "But let's be friends, anyway. I'm Anna Motta-Pia, junior janitor."

I sized her up. Ms. Motta-Pia had the usual buckteeth and nervous nose you come to expect in a bunny. Her bulging eyes were brown as melted fudge, and her ears stood up like two tan ladyfingers.

(Or maybe I was just craving dessert.)

"Uh, Ms. Motta-Pia . . . ," I began.

"Anna, please," she said. "Maureen is out. Y'all come on in."

We followed her into the cramped office. Buckets, mops, brooms, and an army of cleaning products lined the walls. One desk—Ms. DeBree's—was as spotless as a Teflon necktie. The other, smaller desk overflowed with papers, parsley, and a half-eaten carrot.

Anna Motta-Pia hopped onto a stool. "I was fixin' to have a snack. Care for some greens?"

"Only at gunpoint," I said. "No, we're here to investigate a theft."

The bunny's eyes grew big. "Oh, no."

"Oh, yes," said Natalie. "A pearl necklace was stolen."

"Mercy!" said Anna. Her nose twitched like a mischief-maker in the principal's office. "Right here at Emerson Hicky?"

"Yep," I said. "And we're trying to find out who did it." I leaned on her desk.

"Heavens to Flopsy!" said the rabbit. Her eyes flicked to a photo on the wall that showed about twenty bunnies in two rows.

"Your football team?" I asked.

"My family," she said. "But a theft, here? Maureen will be fit to be tied."

"It probably happened at recess, when the door was locked," said Natalie.

I nodded at a fat ring of keys hanging from a hook. "Who has keys to the first-grade classrooms?"

Anna nibbled the flower in the buttonhole of her

overalls. "Well...Maureen and I, of course. Then, the teachers, and...I don't rightly know who-all. The front-office folks?"

"Could anyone just slip in here and lift those keys?" I asked.

"Mercy no!" said the rabbit. "They're kept under lock and key—that is, when one of us isn't using them."

"How about the office copies?"

Her nose twitched some more. "You'd have to ask up there."

"We will," said Natalie.

Anna held up a furry finger. "I bet someone swiped the teacher's keys. I bet you anything!"

I eased up off the desk. "Leave the detecting to us, Anna. We private eyes try not to jump to conclusions until we have all the facts."

She hopped to her feet. "Ah, well, I'm sure y'all know best."

"That's what he keeps telling his mom," said Natalie. "But she still doesn't believe him."

3

I, Chihuahua

Detectives have to knock on a lot of doors in the course of an investigation. No big deal. It's all in a day's work.

Unless we're knocking on the big red door that opens into Principal Zero's office.

A huge tomcat with a hair-trigger temper, Mr. Zero has munched up and spit out more tough guys than a champion gumchewer at a bubble-blowing contest.

This gecko doesn't like getting his tail chomped. That's why I always check instead with the secretary, Mrs. Maggie Crow.

When Natalie and I reached the office, we had to take a number. The black bird was already juggling two unhappy customers.

"No, I must see him now," said the first, a jumpy Chihuahua. "This just won't do."

Mrs. Crow narrowed her eyes. "Look, Miss Flemm, it ain't gonna happen. He's with the superintendent."

Miss Flemm? I muttered to Natalie, "That's Pinky's teacher."

"Sometimes we're good," she said. "Sometimes we're lucky."

The second visitor butted in. "You don't understaaand," whined the little alligator lizard. "Somebody stole my dad's watch from my desk."

"Yeah, yeah," Mrs. Crow rasped.

"If I don't get it back, he'll killll me."

Mrs. Crow looked as if she wouldn't mind that one bit. "I said I'd tell the principal when he's free. Now, beat it."

Hmm . . . another theft? I waggled my eyebrows at Natalie.

She nodded. When the lizard shuffled out of the room, she followed.

"Honestly, Mrs. Crow," huffed the Chihuahua, "I must get some action on this right away. Classroom thefts cannot stand unpunished."

I edged forward. *Had Pinky changed her mind and told Miss Flemm about the missing necklace?*

The crow toyed with a shiny ring. "Sorry you mislaid your tiara," she said.

"It was *stolen*," said Miss Flemm, "from a locked room."

"Whatever," said Mrs. Crow. "Look, unless somebody's actually lost a limb or been snatched by aliens, I ain't opening that door."

"But—"

"I'll tell him when he comes out," said the crow. "Now why don't you get back to your kids before they steal your whole classroom."

The Chihuahua's eyes grew wider than the waistband of a hippo's undershorts. "They wouldn't—would they?" She trotted out the door.

I leaned on the counter. "Mrs. Crow, is it possible that someone could steal the office keys without you knowing?"

The big bird snorted. Her snort turned into a cackle, and the cackle into a cough.

"That's what I thought," I said.

Scooting out the door, I caught up with Pinky's teacher. "Miss Flemm?"

She turned her head, but didn't slow down. "Yes? Who are you?"

"Chet Gecko. Pinky's brother." Tipping my hat, I gave her my Number Two Friendliest Grin. I let my reputation do the rest.

"Oh," she said. "You."

Unfortunately, my reputation had preceded me.

"I hear your tiara went missing," I said. "Maybe

my keen detective skills can help you find it." I was polite. I didn't even ask what the heck a teacher was doing with a tiara.

She paused. "I'm listening."

"Was it stolen during recess?"

"Why, yes."

"And you're sure you had the room key with you at all times?" I asked.

Miss Flemm patted her flowered purse. "Always," she said. "This never leaves my arm."

"Could someone have taken the key from your purse?"

"Not likely," said Miss Flemm. "Just try it—go ahead."

I snaked my hand between the straps and started into the bag.

Snap!

The sides of the purse chomped together like a hungry shark's jaws, narrowly missing my fingers.

"Yikes!" I cried, cradling my hand. "That's some security system."

"The Little Nipper. *Nobody* steals from my purse," the Chihuahua growled. She continued walking.

Tagging along, I said, "Then the thief broke in?"

She sniffed. "No, and the door was locked when I returned from recess."

We had nearly reached the first-grade building. "One last thing?" I asked.

"Make it snappy," said Miss Flemm.

"About your students," I said. "Any sticky-fingered ones?"

She put a paw to the doorknob and turned. "Certainly not. These are well-behaved, obedient boys and girls."

And with that, she opened the door and stepped into pandemonium. Kids were flying paper airplanes, chasing one another, dancing on desks, and laughing.

"Everybody in your seats," the dog barked. "Now!"

As the door closed, startled kids dived for their chairs.

Ah, dear old first grade. I missed it. Like a case of chicken pox.

I caught up with Natalie at the edge of the playground. She was chatting with a fluffy owl.

"Got a minute?" I asked.

"For you?" she said. "Even more. Sixty whole seconds. See ya, Madison!"

The owl waved and fluttered off.

"So, what did you find out?" I asked.

"Plenty." She grinned. "Madison says the school fair will have a kissing booth, hayrides, cotton candy, maybe even clowns—"

My face froze. "Not clowns."

"What's wrong with clowns?"

"Uh, nothing," I said, suppressing a shudder. "I just don't like 'em, that's all."

Natalie cocked her head. "Looks like someone's got a case of Bozo-phobia."

"What's that?"

"Uncontrollable fear of clowns," she said.

I forced a laugh. "Don't be a sap. Now can we get back to the *case,* worm-brain? What did you find out?"

"Oh, that. The alligator lizard said his dad's digital watch was stolen from his desk at recess."

"And? Is he in Pinky's class?"

"Nope," said Natalie, grooming her feathers. "He's in another room."

I stroked my chin. "Hmm. So we've got a busy little thief."

"Or *thieves,*" she said.

"Birdie," I said. "You know just how to cheer up a private eye."

She lifted a shoulder. "It's a gift."

"Now, why don't we—"

The class bell rang. While it may be true that crime never stops, detective work sometimes does. I shook my head and tromped back to class.

It ain't easy being a grade-school PI.

4

Bad Coon Rising

You've heard that absence makes the heart grow fonder? Not true. After spending lunchtime away from our sour substitute, I wasn't any fonder of her than I had been in the morning.

I suffered through her lessons anyhow. And when late recess rolled around, I led the charge for the door.

Natalie caught up with me at our unofficial office, the scrofulous tree.

"Time to compare notes," I said, patting the space beside me.

She cocked her head. "Are we talking about your fake excuse notes, or notes on the case?"

"The case, funny bird. What's the *what*?"

"What?"

"The *what*," I said. "Like who, what, when, where, why? What've we got so far?"

Natalie settled in on a tree root. "Let's see, at recess, some kid—"

"Or teacher," I said.

"Stole your sister's pearls, the lizard's watch, and Miss Whosit's tiara."

"From two different rooms." I cupped my chin in my hands and stared up into the tree's scraggly leaves. "Hmm. That's *when* and *where*. So what's the *why*?"

"Someone wants to look pretty while telling time?" said Natalie.

We chewed this over. "Nah," we said together. Natalie stretched a wing. "So how about the *who*?"

"The what?"

"The *who*," she said. "Who's the logical suspect when something goes missing at Emerson Hicky?"

We looked at each other.

"Duh," I said, hitting my head. "Johnny Ringo. Why didn't I think of it sooner?"

"Because you needed my superior brainpower?" she said with a grin.

I gave her a look. "Smugness is so unattractive in a private eye."

Johnny Ringo was a plump raccoon with a fondness for the finer things—especially the finer things that didn't belong to him. He was smoother than silverfish butter and slicker than a sackful of eels in olive oil.

Johnny Ringo was the black heart of Emerson Hicky's black market.

This wheeler-dealer usually wheeled and dealt at the playground's edge with his beefy wolverine sidekick. (And you *really* don't want to get kicked in the side by that guy, I can tell you.)

Sure enough, we found the raccoon moving hot goods underneath some oak trees. As we approached, a blue jay stuffed something into his book bag.

"And there's more where that came from," Johnny said.

The bird spotted us. "Yeah, uh, thanks." He flapped off in a hurry.

"Hey, Johnny," I said. "How's tricks?"

He grinned and spread his paws. "Tricks are for kids, amigo. Listen, you wanna go stand over by the sandbox? You're bad for business."

"Funny," I said, crossing my arms. "Business is just what we came to talk about."

Natalie scanned the area. "Where's your friend?"

"Rolf?" said Johnny Ringo. He glanced at his digital watch. "On coffee break. Get to the point. You're burning up daylight."

"Nice watch," I said. "The point is this: A pearl necklace went missing today."

The raccoon inspected me with his mild, amused eyes. "So? Stuff vanishes all the time."

"And a lot of it vanishes into your paws," said Natalie.

"Rumors, mere rumors," said Johnny Ringo. "I get a bad rap."

"You're a bad raccoon," I said. "Tell me, where were you during the little kids' early recess?"

His ringed tail twitched. "Where I always am, snoop: Ms. Burrower's class."

"Uh-huh," I said, uncrossing my arms. "And you didn't happen to step out for a bathroom break and a bit of light robbery?"

The raccoon bared his teeth. "No way."

Natalie stepped closer to me. "And you didn't pick up a tiara and that nice digital watch while you were snatching the pearl necklace?"

His black eyes turned as hard as an extra-credit math problem. "This is *my* watch, friend. Why do I get blamed for everything that disappears?"

"Beats me," I said. "Is it because you're the biggest thief at school?"

"I didn't come here to be insulted," snarled the raccoon.

"Where do you usually go?" said Natalie.

"That's it!" snapped Johnny Ringo. "Enough of your lip. Sic 'em, Rolf!"

The branches rustled above our heads. I looked up to see a wolverine plummeting, like an emergency airlift of mean and ugly.

"*Yaah!*"

I dodged to one side, Natalie to the other.

Whomp!

Rolf landed between us in a shower of leaves and fur.

"I thought he was on coffee break," said Natalie.

"Sure," said Johnny. "He broke coffee, and now he's gonna break you."

Natalie and I didn't wait for the big lug to recover. We beat feet.

From behind us came Ringo's roar, "Ice those creeps!"

We tore across the open playground, weaving between soccer players and random kids. I risked a glance back.

Rolf came pounding after us, knocking the players aside like Tinkertoys. He was fast for a big guy. And he was gaining.

Natalie took to the sky. "Get the lead out, Gecko!"

"Time for . . . Plan P!" I panted.

"P?" she asked.

"As in *pick up!*" I jumped for her legs and just managed to snag them.

Natalie dipped dangerously. "Let go! You're heavy."

"Not half as heavy as Rolf," I said, hanging on. "Head for that classroom!"

Bobbing and weaving, she flapped for the nearest portable building. We were nearly there.

I looked over my shoulder.

Ringo's goon was mere steps behind us. He grinned, flashing more fangs than a werewolf film festival.

"A couple of sittin' ducks," he chuckled.

"I'm no duck; I'm a *mockingbird!*" cried Natalie.

She was coming in a little too low to make the roof.

"Up, birdie! Up!" I yelled.

We rose, maybe a foot.

The wall rushed to meet me like an eager parent after summer camp.

We weren't going to make it.

I gritted my teeth.

Wham!

I smacked into the wall like a cream pie launched by catapult.

"Oogh," I groaned.

Somehow, I held on. Good ol' sticky gecko feet. I wiggled upward.

The wolverine was jumping at—and just missing—my tail.

"Come back here, ya maroons!" snarled Rolf.

"The word is *moron*," I grunted, "as any moron would know."

Natalie reached down. Between us, we managed to lift me onto the roof.

"Nice flying," I said.

"The flying is fine," said Natalie. "It's the landing you have to watch out for."

"*Now* you tell me, birdie."

5

Shirley, You Jest

A teacher finally came and chased off Rolf. Natalie and I climbed back down. On the way to class, we chewed over what we'd learned so far. It made for a very small snack.

"What do you think about Ringo?" asked Natalie.

"He acted as innocent as a crook can act," I said, rubbing my sore jaw.

"But he's got that watch," she said. "And he's a known liar."

We made our way around a pair of sixth graders— a flying squirrel and a lemming joined at the lips. It gave me the heebie-jeebies. Cootie Central.

"Truth is, you can't trust a liar," I said.

Natalie cocked her head. "But if you can't trust a liar to always lie, then he *could* be telling the truth."

"Huh?"

"What if he really *didn't* take the pearls?"

I kneaded my forehead. "All this detecting is making my brains hurt."

"Or maybe that's just the portable building," said Natalie.

But a sore head and a jumbled mind weren't the worst in store. When I reached my classroom door, I found myself face-to-face with Shirley Chameleon.

"Oh, hiii, Chet," she said with a giggle.

"Shirley." I tried to step around her.

She blocked me with her tail. "Thanks for taking the heat."

"What do you mean?"

Shirley batted her big green googly eyes. "You didn't tell on me—even though Ms. Dwyer punished you."

"I tried, but she didn't give me half a chance," I said.

"So . . . ," said Shirley.

"So?"

She fiddled with her scarf. "Have you thought anymore about what I asked you?"

My palms got sweaty. "About the, uh, dance?"

"Yeeesss," Shirley breathed. "Will you go with me?"

"Okay," I said.

"Really?"

I nodded. "Sure. When chipmunks fly and elephants play the tuba."

She pouted, and I pushed past her into the classroom. *Sheesh.* What's a guy gotta do to shake these dizzy dames?

After school, I loitered around Pinky's classroom. It riled me that I was no closer to catching the thief. So I figured I'd get back to basics, maybe search the other kids' desks for my mom's necklace.

I figured wrong.

"What are *you* doing here?" asked Miss Flemm.

"Detecting," I said. "It's what detectives do. Want me to look for your missing tiara?"

The Chihuahua sniffed. "Do you take me for a total fool?"

"Well, maybe not a *total*—"

"Do you think I haven't already turned this classroom inside out?"

I shook my head. "I don't—"

The Chihuahua stalked toward me, brandishing a plastic rose. "For all *I* know, *you* could be the thief, returning to the scene of the crime."

"Me?"

The last few stragglers in her classroom stopped to stare.

"Get out," yipped Miss Flemm. "Bug off, before I call Mr. Zero."

When a teacher goes bonkers, it's best not to argue. I bugged.

Pinky was waiting by the flagpole, chewing her lip. When I drew near, she jumped up.

"Well?" said Pinky. "Didja find it? Huh?"

"Not yet," I said, "but we're following leads. It'll turn up."

She slumped. "But what if it doesn't?"

"It will."

"But what if you're wrong?"

I spread my arms wide. "Me, the greatest lizard detective at school? I'm never wrong. Cheer up, munchkin."

Pinky gave a shy smile and began to trudge home.

As I followed, the thought struck me: What if I *was* wrong? What if I couldn't find the necklace? Pinky would be crushed.

I shook my head. Why should that bother me? Hard-boiled detectives don't worry about their sisters' feelings. They just knock heads, solve mysteries, take a licking, and keep on ticking.

But that little voice inside wasn't as easy to fool as a little sister.

From a simple case of theft, this was growing into something as challenging as Scrabble in Swahili. And I had a sinking feeling it would only get worse.

6

Snakey Breaky Heart

The next morning, clouds covered the sky, as dark and deep as a bullfrog's belch. It suited my mood to a T.

If you ask me, mornings are a terrible way to start the day. I say we should just jump directly to recess, followed by lunch.

Unfortunately, the principal seldom listens to what I have to say.

On the way to school, I stirred the soggy corn-flakes in that bowl of mush I call my brain. Somewhere out there, a thief was laughing at me. He or she had ripped off my sister, and I hadn't yet caught the creep.

The only saving grace: My mom hadn't noticed her pearl necklace was missing. At least not yet.

A voice broke into my thoughts. "Look out below!"

I glanced up to see Natalie swooping into a two-point landing on the sidewalk. Mockingbirds have some serious moves.

"Hey, private-eye guy," said Natalie. "What's the scoop?"

"Chocolate or pistachio," I said.

She stretched a wing. "Dang. I was hoping for some earthworm ripple. Ready to track down a thief?"

I yawned. "Ready to go back to bed," I said. "But since I'm up, might as well catch a bad guy."

We had almost reached the school grounds. A clamor of voices came from a knot of students and parents near the gate.

"What's the hubbub, bub?" asked Natalie.

"Search me," I said. "Let's go see."

Natalie and I had to use our elbows to clear a path through the crowd. I glimpsed tangled ropes hanging across the gate.

Finally, we popped out in front. Instinctively, I took a step back.

The ropes were snakes.

Nearly a dozen serpents—cobras, pythons, cottonmouths, and so on—had twined themselves around and across the gate, blocking the entrance. A hefty anaconda held two picket signs in her coils: UNFAIR

TO SNAKES and LET OUR KIDS LEARN. (At least, I THINK she was a girl snake. How do you tell for sure?)

She gave us a sarcastic smile and stuck out her forked tongue.

Across from her, a rattler lectured.

"But you won't let *our* kids go here," he yelled, shaking his rattle. "Is that fair?"

"No!" shouted the other serpents.

A voice behind me boomed, "Can it, Percy. You

know that poisonous and constricting snakes aren't allowed here. It's the law."

Principal Zero shouldered his way through the group. His ears were laid back and his eyes were slits. But Percy the rattler didn't seem to care.

"Big Fat Zero," he sneered. "*This* is for your law! *P-too!*" And the rattlesnake hocked a major loogey right onto the pavement at the principal's feet. It bubbled slightly—a poison spitball.

All the serpents hissed.

The huge cat's tail lashed like a crazy, well, snake. "Break this up right now!" said Mr. Zero. "Before the police break it up for you."

The snakes tightened their grip on the fence and one another. They chanted:

> *"Heck no, we won't go*
> *till our kids can come here, yo!"*

I turned to Natalie. "Shakespeare it ain't."

"But it does get the point across," she said.

Sirens wailed. A police van pulled to the curb, and the officers forced their way through. Within minutes, they had wound the serpents around long poles like some strange snack (Snakes on a Stick?) and carried them off to the paddy wagon.

"This isn't the last of it, Zero!" Percy screamed as the cops loaded him in. "Open up to snakes, or I'll make this school pay!"

With a screech of tires and a whiff of burning rubber, the cops took off. Mr. Zero planted his paws on his hips and surveyed the crowd of students.

"Well, what are you all gaping at?" he said. "Get to class!"

When the big cat says get, you get. We got.

———

Schoolwork can really cramp a detective's style. Mr. Ratnose was still out, and Ms. Dwyer was full of more hot air than a volcano's belch. After endless lectures and two pop quizzes, recess at last limped into sight.

Finally I could get some work done.

Natalie met me in the crowded hallway. "You look grumpy," she said.

"This substitute teacher is really griping my grits."

She held up a wing. "I know what'll cheer you up. Knock, knock."

I shook my head. "Can we just work on our case?"

"Who's there," said Natalie, mimicking my voice.

"Panther," she said, and gave me the eye.

"Okay, panther who?" I asked.

"Panther no panth, I'm going swimming!" Natalie cackled so hard, she bumped into a passing armadillo. He promptly curled into a ball and tumbled down the hall.

"Sorry!" she called after him.

I grabbed her shoulder. "Can we get down to business now?"

"Absolutely," she said with a smirk. "Lead on, O Great Detective."

I patrolled the corridors with Natalie, keeping an eye out for suspicious behavior. Maybe the thief would try to strike again, and then we'd nail him.

As we were passing the library, something went, *"Psst!"*

I waved a hand before my face. "Natalie, I told you beans and berries don't mix."

"Wasn't me," she said.

The *"Psst!"* came again, louder. Just ahead, peeking around the corner, was a familiar face: Anna Motta-Pia, junior janitor.

"Over here," she said. "I've got a lead for your case."

We hurried back into the shadow of the library. The rabbit leaned on a rake, looking around nervously.

"About that theft...," said Anna.

"Yes?" asked Natalie.

The rabbit's whiskers twitched. "I figured out someone else who might have a key. Y'all know the new music teacher?"

I crinkled my forehead. "Um, that big kitty who's filling in for Zoomin' Mayta?"

Natalie snapped her wing tip. "He's a lynx," she said. "Gustav Mauler."

"Sho 'nuff," said the rabbit. "Music teachers have a key to every classroom, 'cause they teach all over school."

"Hmm," I said.

Anna lowered her voice to a whisper. *"And he's*

always pussyfooting around the halls when every-body's at lunch or recess."

Natalie cocked her head. "But why would a music teacher steal?"

"They don't get paid diddly-poo," said the custodian. "Hardly enough to keep them in bow wax and trumpet polish."

My eyes met Natalie's. "Sounds like a motive to me," I said, my spirits rising. "Thanks, Anna. You're a peach."

Before we could hoof it, the rabbit caught my sleeve. "Chet, I'd druther you didn't let Mr. Mauler know you heard it from me. Rabbits and lynxes, we're like Yankees and Rebels."

I crisscrossed my lips with a finger. "Mum's the word, ma'am. Let's go, Natalie."

We prowled the halls, on the lookout for a big old lynx. Third-grade classrooms...nope. Second-grade classrooms...nada.

Near the fourth-grade building, we struck pay dirt. "Mauler at two o'clock," I muttered to Natalie.

"But Chet," she said, "it's only ten thirty."

I rolled my eyes. "Not the time, birdie, the *position*. Twelve o'clock is straight ahead; two o'clock is a bit to the right."

She looked over at me. "Sometimes you say the weirdest things."

We pulled back behind the corner to spy on Mr. Gustav Mauler. Anna was right—he was lurking. Twice he edged up to Ms. Reckonwith's locked door, and twice backed away when someone passed.

Was the lynx working up his nerve to break in?

We'd never know for sure, because Waldo the furball chose that exact moment to blow our cover.

"Hey, it's Chet and Natalie!" he cried. "Working hard, or hardly working? *Hur, hur, hur.*"

I raised a finger to my lips. Too late.

The lynx had spotted us. He stalked up the hall, oozing menace. Mauler's scowl was dark enough to cause a rainstorm in the Sahara, and his fangs twinkled in that special, so-pleased-to-bite-you way.

He loomed over us. "And vhat," asked Gustav Mauler, "are *you* up to?"

7

The Missing Lynx

Waldo gulped. His eyes bugged out like baseballs in a sock.

"Vell?" rumbled Mr. Mauler. "Vhat are you doing?"

"The Hokey Pokey," I said, sticking my right foot in and shaking it all about. "What are *you* doing?"

Gustav Mauler snarled. As snarls go, it was pretty convincing. He looked tougher than Bulgarian algebra and deadlier than a poot in a sleeping bag.

"Since vhen is dot your business?" he said. "I'm de teacher; you're de student."

I eyed his burly frame. "If *you're* a music teacher, I'm Mother Goose."

"You tink I cannot giff you detention?" he

growled. "Vould you like to go to de playground now, or vould you like to find out?"

Waldo tugged on my sleeve. "Playground?" he said. "Pretty please?"

The lynx extended a thick arm and pointed. "Get lost."

I tipped my hat, and we ambled off. "Interesting," I said to Natalie once we were out of earshot.

"Very," she said.

Waldo blinked at us. "Is detective work always this scary? If it is, I don't want to play anymore."

I turned to Natalie. "Let's be thankful for small favors."

Back in class, our substitute flapped her gums about earth science, while I gazed at the blackboard, unseeing. My mind was farther away than a summer vacation on Neptune.

What path should we try next? Mr. Mauler seemed to be hiding something, but then, so did Johnny Ringo. Was one of them the thief?

The porcupine gabbed. I mused. Maybe I was on the wrong track. Maybe I should be finding witnesses instead of grilling suspects. . . .

The sound of my own name broke into my thoughts.

Ms. Dwyer was giving me the fish eye. "You *are* Chet Gecko, aren't you?"

"Uh, last time I checked."

"Then why don't you tell us all about earth tremors?"

I scratched my chin. "Um...well, I do know one thing about 'em. I know what happens to cows in an earthquake."

"What's that?" she asked.

"They give milk shakes," I said.

My classmates' chuckles were chopped off by the porcupine's glare. Her beady-eyed gaze returned to me. "Are you looking for trouble?"

"Nope," I said. "But it comes whether I look or not."

"If you can't speak respectfully, I'm sending you to the principal's office."

I shrugged. "Might as well. I'm not getting much done here."

"That's it!" Ms. Dwyer's quills bristled like an attack cactus. "You're getting double homework."

"*Double!?* But I've got real work to do!"

She scribbled on a pink pad and thrust the note at me. "Go see Mr. Zero right now."

I bit back a smart remark, took the slip, and shuffled out the door.

The halls echoed with the cries of little kids on

their lunch break. I brightened. Maybe I could do some investigating on my way to being punished.

Halfway to the office, I spotted my sister playing with two other munchkins out on the grass.

"Pinky!" I called.

Her head went up, and her eyes got big. She trotted over.

"Chet!" she said. "You found it!"

"Not yet, runt," I said.

Pinky's chin quivered. "But... but what if Mom needs the necklace for her party tomorrow?"

"No worries," I said. "I'll find it long before then."

She gave me a tiny, hopeful smile.

I pasted on a confident grin. But inside, I was plenty worried. A hard-bitten detective hates to admit it, but it's nice to have someone who looks up to you. And I didn't want to see Pinky's trust turn to disgust.

Even if she was my bratty little sister.

"Tell your friends to come over," I said. "I want to ask them about the thefts."

But just then, a flying squirrel with a hall monitor's badge barreled up to us. "What are you doing here, girlie?" she said around a huge wad of gum. "Get back out on the playground. Scat!"

Pinky hightailed it onto the grass.

I checked out the squirrel. She was the same critter I'd seen earlier, swapping spit with another sixth grader.

Loose flaps of skin hung between her front and back legs like a furry cape. The chewing gum pushed her cheeks into balloons, and her black beret, the hall monitor's uniform, dipped at a dangerous angle. Her badge read: LUZ LIPPS.

She noticed my inspection. "Take a picture," said Luz. "It'll last longer."

"Shucks," I said. "And me with no camera."

"So." She popped the gum. "What's *your* business?"

"Monkey business," I said, and waved my pink slip.

The squirrel scowled. "You better get your tail up to the office."

I bowed. "When you put it so sweetly, how can I refuse?"

With a last tough-gal look, she swaggered off down the hall. I made my way to the principal's office.

As always, Mrs. Crow sat at her station. I don't think I'd recognize her without the counter covering half of her body.

"Well, well," she croaked. "To what do I owe this honor?"

I flashed the note. "To my big mouth."

"Now there's a surprise."

"Is Mr. Wonderful in?" I asked.

"Whaddaya know?" said Mrs. Crow. "He is. I'm sure he'd love to see you."

If Mr. Zero felt something when he saw me, it probably wasn't love. It was something cold and hard, with more teeth in it. Squaring my shoulders, I padded across the reception area and up to the half-open red door.

In answer to my knock, a smooth voice purred, "Come in, Gecko."

I trudged up to the wide black desk. Behind it, Emerson Hicky's fearless leader was sharpening his claws on the office drapes. I knew how they felt.

"What is it this time?" said the massive tomcat, turning to face me.

I plunked the pink slip onto his desk. "The substitute doesn't like me."

"Imagine that," he rumbled, and scanned the note.

"In my defense, let me say I was working on a case."

"Mister, you *are* a case." He smoothed his whiskers. "You're nothing but trouble, you avoid your schoolwork, and you have a bad attitude. And do you know what I plan do about it?"

I braced myself. "What?"

His fangs glinted in a smile. "Hire you."

You could've knocked me over with a hummingbird feather.

8

Boy Meets Squirrel

"Uh..." I gaped. "You, uh, want to hire me?"

Mr. Zero leaned onto his forearms. "Gecko, despite all your faults, you actually have solved a case or two."

"Gee, thanks," I said.

The principal's claws emerged. His eyes narrowed. "And now I've got a case that needs solving. Things have begun disappearing around school."

Yeah, like my mom's necklace, I thought.

"At first, we didn't worry much—a watch here, a camera there. But last night, two computers went missing from the library."

I whistled. "Them's big potatoes. Any clues?"

Mr. Zero's claws sank into his scarred desktop.

"None," he rumbled. "No sign of a break-in; no evidence left behind."

"Impressive," I said. "This operation is slicker than greased duck snot."

The principal raised an eyebrow.

"If you'll, uh, pardon the phrase," I said.

"I want you to help me shut down this thief," he said. "Pronto."

I spread my hands. "I'm flattered, boss man. Lil' old me? But why haven't you called in John Q. Law—you know, the cops?"

"You're suspicious for a fourth grader."

"It's a suspicious world," I said.

The principal tilted back and rubbed his watermelon gut with a paw. He seemed to be chewing something over.

"Very well," he said. "We can't call the police because I don't want any word of this to get out."

"Afraid it'll scare off the tourists?" I asked.

"No, Gecko. If the school superintendent hears that we've got thieves, he won't let us display the Flubberjee Egg."

I blinked. "The who-bejee what?"

His eyebrows drew together like two caterpillars smooching. "Do you pay *any* attention to what happens at this school?"

"As little as possible."

"The egg is a rare jewel being shown at the fair tomorrow. If the super hears we've got a theft problem, he won't let it come here."

I scratched my chin. "And this would be a problem because . . . ?"

He leaned forward. "No egg, no big crowds. No big crowds, no big money for our fund-raiser. Get it?"

"Got it."

"Good," he said. "Catch the thief before the fair."

I tilted my hat back. "If I do, what's in it for me?"

"I look the other way the next three times you get in trouble."

"And if I don't catch him?" I asked.

Quick as a cop on a doughnut, Mr. Zero's paw shot out. His razor claws shredded my pink slip.

"Do I make myself clear?" he growled.

"As a poltergeist's X-ray."

"Then I suggest you hop to it."

I may not be a bunny, but I know a good idea when I hear it. Out the door I hopped.

Suddenly, our case had mushroomed from something personal to something that affected the whole school. The pressure was on. Come lunchtime, I tore through my brown-bag lunch like a shark through a goldfish picnic.

Natalie watched me. "Are we in a race?" she said, pecking at her wormy apple crisp.

"A race against time," I said. "Principal Zero has hired us."

She brightened. "How about that?"

"Yeah, and if we don't catch the thief by tomorrow afternoon, it's curtains for this gecko."

"Curtains? Good. You really need to redecorate your office."

"Mr. Zero will redecorate *me*," I said. "Scarf down that mess, and let's skedaddle."

Natalie gave a few more pecks at her lunch, and then tossed the rest. I swear she eats like a bird.

"Let's review our suspects," I said as we hit the bricks.

"Right," she said. "There's Johnny Ringo . . ."

"Who swears he was in class but always lies. Then, there's Gustav Mauler . . ."

Natalie nodded. "Who roams the halls at recess. Anyone else?"

I paused at the edge of the playground. "What about those snake protesters?"

"What about them?"

"Snakes are sneaky. They could be stealing things."

Natalie bristled. "That's prejudice! There are good snakes and bad snakes, just like with any animal— even geckos."

I screwed up my face. "I still don't trust them."

"How could they be behind it?" demanded Natalie. "That rattler only made his threat this morning—*after* all the thefts happened."

"Ah," I said. "So, scratch the snakes."

"I'd rather not," she said.

I smirked. "Now who's prejudiced?"

Natalie ignored me. "Which suspect shall we start with?"

"Well..." I thought about using the *eenie-meenie-miney-moe* technique, but it didn't seem very detective-y. Just then, a muskrat in a hall monitor's black beret marched down the corridor behind us.

I smiled. "Let's see if we can find a witness first," I said.

Natalie followed my gaze. "A hall monitor?"

"You read my mind, birdie."

The muskrat hadn't seen anything suspicious, but he told us to check with Luz Lipps. I thanked him for his time. He asked me for a tip. I told him not to bet on horses. He said not that kind of tip.

We spotted Luz in the library corridor. As we approached, she was pulling back from a weasel's embrace. *Yuck.* If this dame was half as good a monitor as she was a flirt, Emerson Hicky would have the calmest halls in the county.

At the sight of us, the squirrel gave a guilty start.

She released the weasel. "And don't, uh, run in the halls again," she said to him. "If you know what's good for you."

He shot her a puzzled look and shuffled off.

"Remind me never to run in the halls," I said. "Luz, I'm Chet; this is my partner, Natalie. We met before."

"Big whoop," she said around a huge chaw in her cheek. "What do you want?"

We joined the squirrel. "We're investigating a case," said Natalie.

"A case of what? Soda pop?" Luz smirked.

"Theft," I said, leaning close. "Hadn't you heard?"

The squirrel jumped, nearly choking on her gum. "Theft?"

"Someone's been stealing watches and other stuff from classrooms at recess," said Natalie.

"And yesterday, they boosted a couple of computers," I said. "Know anything about it?"

Luz glanced down the hall and back at us. "Why should I?" she demanded. "Uh, I mean, why would *I* know anything about that?"

I stuffed my hands into my pockets. "You *are* a hall monitor. Don't you monitor the halls?"

"Maybe you noticed someone shady," Natalie suggested.

The squirrel's face shut down tighter than a

candy store on Sunday. "Uh, nobody I can remember. Look, I'm kinda busy . . ."

I swept an arm out. "Go," I said. "Monitorize. But if you think of any—"

"I'll let you know," Luz interrupted. "Now I gotta— Hey, you! I saw you drop that candy wrapper!" She hustled off after a litterbug.

"Anything strike you as suspicious?" asked Natalie.

"Other than the shifty gaze, the quick change of subject, and the rushing away?" I said. "Nothing. Why do you ask?"

"I think we should keep an eye on Luz Lipps."

"Fair enough," I said. "But we're using *your* eye."

9

Clue in the Face

Sometimes being a detective is a bit like being a baker. A private eye has to take the slimmest of leads and weave a whole case from it. (Okay, maybe it's more like being a rug maker. But you get the picture. Detecting is hard.)

After a side trip to the snack machine for a Pillbug Crunch bar, Natalie and I decided to follow our slim lead and do some hall monitoring of our own.

The corridors were mostly deserted. We spotted Anna Motta-Pia sweeping. She glanced up, startled, and then gave us a friendly wave.

The next two hallways were as quiet as a whisper at midnight. But over by the third-grade building Natalie and I caught a break.

As we rounded the corner, a stealthy movement captured my eye. Two rooms down, a big furry someone was fiddling with a doorknob.

We ducked behind a trash can. When I poked my nose around the edge, I saw . . .

"Mr. Mauler!" whispered Natalie.

"Sneaking into a classroom."

The big lynx opened the door and glanced up and down the hall.

We pulled back behind the can. A soft *click* sounded. I looked again, and the music teacher had slipped inside.

"Something's fishy," said Natalie.

"As a dolphin's dinner," I agreed. "Let's go take a peek."

"Are you nuts?" she hissed. "He'll spot us."

I jerked a thumb at my chest. "Not this wall crawler. You coming?"

Natalie shook her head.

Moving as quietly as a mouse at catnap time, I scaled the wall. When I was just below the windows of the room Mr. Mauler had entered, I slowly raised my head to peer inside.

A hideous, mutant face stared into mine.

I gasped.

Then I relaxed. It was a drawing—a lame drawing, at that. The teacher had taped her students' artwork into every other pane. I slipped over to the next window and pressed my face to the glass.

Gustav Mauler was just closing the desk drawer. His back was half turned, so I couldn't tell what he was doing. But it seemed like he slipped a paw into his vest.

What was the wildcat up to?

Finished, Mr. Mauler turned and made for the door.

Whoops. No time to run.

As he reached for the knob, the lynx started to look toward my window. Quick as a flash, I made the most revolting face I could, and froze.

Mr. Mauler flinched. "Ug-*ly,*" he muttered. "And dey call dot *art.*"

He slipped through the door below me. I held still, praying that he wouldn't look up again.

My luck held. The door shut, and footfalls padded down the corridor.

my sistun

"Okay," whispered Natalie after a few moments. "He's gone."

I scrambled down. "Caught him red-handed," I said.

"What did he steal?" asked Natalie.

"I'm not sure, but he was red-handed. That might be the wrong-o who ripped off my sister. Let's catch up to him."

We hotfooted it down the hall.

The lynx must have picked up his pace. We caught a glimpse of a bobbed tail as he slipped around the next corner.

"Hurry!" cried Natalie.

"*Hurry* is my middle name," I said.

"I thought it was Rambo."

I broke into a jog. "Less chat, more hustle."

But by the time we passed the next building, Gustav Mauler was nowhere to be seen.

"Dang!" I said.

Natalie and I patrolled the corridor, heads swiveling. Across the grass, we spotted a line of snakes pressed to the school fence in silent protest. But no kitty. Mr. Mauler had given us the slip.

Our feet led us at last to the library.

I scratched my head. "Now, where did that cat scat to?"

"Search me," said Natalie. "But weren't the computers stolen from the library?"

"Yeah."

She grinned. "Then what say we stop and look for one of those . . . what do you detectives call them? Chews? Gnus?"

"Clues," I said.

"Let's cruise."

Natalie and I pushed through the heavy oak doors into the cool quiet of the library. It smelled of old books, confusion, and fancy-schmancy coffee. Cool Beans, the librarian, held the coffee. The book smell came from, no duh, the books.

And I'm not sure where the confusion came from. (Maybe me.)

"Hey, Cool Beans," I said.

The hefty possum looked up from his cup of java. "What's shakin', private eyes?"

"Nothing but the knees of the bad guys," I said.

"Or their bellies, from laughing," said Natalie.

Cool Beans gazed at us through his wraparound shades. "The word is, you're lookin' into some light-fingered Louies around campus."

"Word travels fast," I said. "What can you tell us about the computer theft?"

The possum sipped his coffee. "Happened after I split yesterday. When I dropped in to work this A.M., I found that space"—he pointed at the gap in his line of computers—"where two machines should have been."

I strolled over to see. "And they didn't break in?"

"Nah, those sneaky squares must have had a key."

Natalie joined me and eyeballed the computer table. "Any clues?"

"No muddy footprints, no bloody handkerchiefs, no bad-guy library cards," said Cool Beans.

I shook my head. "I was afraid of that."

"But outside the window," he said, "I did find *this*." The possum held up something that looked like a see-through scrap of parchment.

"Paper?" I said. "This place is lousy with it."

"Guess again, Sherlock. Snakeskin."

My eyes met Natalie's. "And where there's snake-skin . . . ," I said.

"There's snakes," she finished.

I grinned. "Hey, great minds think alike."

"Or as my mom says, fools seldom differ."

10

Iguana Hold Your Hand

After talking with Cool Beans, we still had more questions than answers. But I'm used to that. The same thing happens half the time I take a test.

Natalie and I stepped out into the bright sunshine.

"How'd we get so many suspects?" I said, ticking them off on my fingers. "I count Mr. Mauler, Johnny Ringo, Luz Lipps, and some mystery snake."

"So which one did it?" asked Natalie.

"Beats me, but when I catch that thief..."

Natalie led the way down the corridor. "Maybe we should try eliminating them one by one. Then whoever's left will be the culprit."

"Alrighty," I said, "Time for some shadow work."

Natalie clapped her wings together. "Oh, goodie.

I always wanted to learn how to make those little bunny rabbit shapes."

"Not shadow puppets, *shadowing*." I gave her a look. "You know, following suspects around to see what you can find out? Dang, birdie, you still—"

She grinned. "Gotcha! I swear, Chet, you are *so* gullible sometimes."

"I must be," I said. "I have you for a partner."

When we reached a crossroads, Natalie stopped. "How about if I look for Mr. Mauler?"

"Then I'll take Luz Lipps," I said, heading down the right-hand hall. "We'll talk at the next recess."

"Okeydokey, artichokey," she called.

"In an hour, cauliflower," I said.

Lunch period was disappearing faster than the last slurps of a millipede root beer float. I stepped up my pace, checking each corridor for the flying squirrel.

And then I found her. Hugging the wall, I watched as a boy walked up to Luz. They chatted briefly and leaned close—too close. Not again!

My face screwed up in disgust, and I turned away.

When I looked back, the two had separated, and the boy was strolling off. Luz started toward me, her cheeks puffed out. How had she managed her gum during the lip-lock? I wondered.

Then I realized I really didn't want to know.

The flying squirrel stopped dead, staring right at me.

Dang.

Distracted, I had forgotten the first rule of shadowing: Stay hidden.

I stepped out. "Luz, can you tell me—" I began.

The hall monitor spun and hurried off in the other direction. Her loose skin folds fluttered like a furry bathrobe.

"Was it something I said?" I hustled after her.

Luz broke into that hopping run that squirrels favor. I poured on the steam.

Suddenly, a teacher appeared beyond her. "No running here!" he cried.

Luz skidded to a stop and glanced back at me. Pinned between us, she took the high road—right up the wall.

But she'd forgotten about my serious climbing skills. In this business, it pays to be a lizard.

I scrambled up the wall in pursuit. When I reached the roof, Luz was already hop-running away. I took off, pumping my legs like a cancan dancer on a bathroom run.

Within a few strides, I was gaining. The edge of the building lay just ahead.

Luz looked back, panic flaring in her eyes.

I reached out my arms, almost close enough to grab her.

Luz was only steps from the drop-off. She had nowhere to go. . . .

Until she stepped into space, spread her arms and legs, and sailed away.

Turns out I'd forgotten something, too: Flying squirrels can fly.

With the grace of a prima ballerina, Luz landed on the next building's roof.

Unfortunately, geckos can't glide.

I windmilled off the edge.

"Yaaaah!"

Down I plummeted like a cast-iron kite—*krunk!*—right into the krangleberry bushes.

I lay there for a minute. Nothing seemed broken, so I rose and picked my way out of the shrubbery.

A slow *clap-clap-clap* greeted me.

Two beefy iguanas stood nearby. One had a squinchy left eye; the other had a nose ring. Neither was about to win any beauty contests. They looked like trouble, and they smelled like algae.

Squinchy Eye stopped his applause. "Lovely jump," he said, "but you didn't stick the landing, mate. I'd give it a seven-point-five."

"Oy'd say free-point-two," said Nose Ring. And his glower made it clear he was being generous.

I brushed the leaves off my coat. "Thanks for the warm fuzzies," I said. "See you gents later."

But I hadn't taken two steps before Nose Ring blocked my way.

"Not so fast," he growled.

"I know you're not, but what am I?" I said.

"Unh?"

The hefty reptile knew he'd been insulted, but he couldn't quite figure out how. He grabbed the front of my coat in a hamlike fist and hoisted me off the ground, easy as a high schooler popping a zit.

"Listen up, Gecko," said Squinchy Eye. "We don't like you. It ain't personal, but we don't like you."

"Aw, that breaks my heart," I said. "And just when I was about to give you a best-friends-forever bracelet."

Nose Ring raised a hand the size of a three-ring binder and slapped my head once, twice, three times. Church bells chimed in my ears.

"'E said, *listen up,*" said the iguana.

Squinchy Eye bent down until his squinchy eye was only inches from mine. His breath smelled funkier than the morning after the fish tank office party.

"We got a message for you, bright boy," he said.

"Send an e-mail next ti—" I stopped at the sight of Nose Ring's raised hand.

"Get outta town, mate," said Squinchy Eye. "Emerson Hicky don't want you around no more."

I gulped. "I don't want Emerson Hicky, either," I said. "But until I graduate from sixth grade, I'm stuck here."

"Wrong answer," said Nose Ring. He hoisted

me over his head, planted a meaty paw in my gut, and shot-putted me back into the bushes.

Cha-krunk!

"Sweet," said Squinchy Eye. "I'd give it a nine-point-seven."

"'Leven-point-two," grunted the other iguana.

"It only goes up to ten." Squinchy Eye peered down at me through the shrubbery. "Lay off the case, Gecko. Or we'll have to lay you out."

I didn't have any snappy answers for that one. Instead, I felt my lumps and bruises, and listened to their footsteps retreat.

Goons giving me heat? That meant I was getting close to something big.

Only question was, would I find it before something big came down on me?

11

Another Day, Another Mauler

The stretch between lunch and recess didn't last longer than the day before summer vacation, Dad's "when I was a boy" lectures, or the Hundred Years' War.

It just felt that way.

When the recess bell rang, I disappeared from the classroom like allowance money at the mall. This case was getting tangled. It would take Natalie's and my brainpower, plus a jumbo pair of scissors, to cut through the kinks.

We met at the swings. I was taking this case too personally, and I needed to get my head straight. Sometimes the motion helps loosen up my thinking. (And sometimes it's just fun to swing.)

As we swung, I gave Natalie the scoop on my lunchtime adventures.

"So Luz took off?" she said. "Sure sounds like she's guilty of something."

"Of flying in the halls, at the very least," I said, pulling on the chains.

Natalie rushed past me. "But who sicced those two goons on you? Luz?"

"Or someone else I've been bugging."

She grinned. "How to choose? There are so many."

"It's my natural charm," I said, whooshing forward. "Which reminds me: What happened with you and our charming lynx friend?"

Natalie bailed out at the top, spread her wings, and glided down to the sand.

Show-off.

"I followed Mr. Mauler down the halls," she said. "First, he slipped into another classroom. And then he went and stood outside the teachers' lounge, peering through the window."

"Huh," I said. "That's . . ." I zoomed forward. At the height of my arc, I let go and tucked into a ball.

One flip, two flips . . .

Ker-whomp!

Belly flop.

"Interesting," I wheezed.

Natalie helped me up. "Stick with detecting," she said. "And leave flying to the birds and the squirrels."

"What was Mr. Mauler up to at the teachers' lounge?" I wondered. "Checking if the coast was clear for stealing?"

Natalie shrugged. "So what next, Mr. PI? The lady or the lynx?"

I hoofed it for the hallways. "The lady," I said. "She's hiding something, and with a little pressure, we can squeeze it out of her."

But before we could find the squirrel, I came in for some pressure of my own.

A hulking shape stepped from the shadows of the first building.

Principal Zero.

"Did you kiddies have fun on the swings?" he purred.

"Sure did," said Natalie. "We—"

"That's nice," said the big cat. "While you were lollygagging, we had another theft—a pair of diamond earrings from Ms. Glick's desk."

"Uh-oh," I said.

"*Uh-oh* is right," said Mr. Zero. His tail began to twitch—never a good sign. "Have you identified the thief yet?"

I studied a clump of grass. "Er, no, but we've got a couple of solid leads."

The principal bent close. His tuna-fish breath surrounded me like a cloud. "Then follow them," he said. "Tick-tock, Gecko. The fair is tomorrow. Time's a-wasting."

And with a farewell glare, Big Fat Zero turned and stalked away.

"Nothing like a little pep talk to get us motivated," said Natalie.

"You're right," I said. "That was nothing like a little pep talk."

We patrolled the halls with a new sense of urgency. But Luz Lipps was harder to find than an I LOVE BULLIES button in a herd of nerds. We searched on.

Passing near the office, we spotted a familiar face on the other side of the school fence: Percy, the feisty rattlesnake from that morning's protest. And he was talking with Johnny Ringo.

They gave us the hairy eyeball as we walked by.

"I don't trust that sidewinder," I said.

"Which one?" asked Natalie.

"Take your pick. Either one of them could be behind the thefts."

She glanced back. "Shall we spy?"

"Let's split up. You watch these creeps; I'll track down Luz."

But after combing my way through the school

and back again, I came up Luz-less. I stopped to slurp some water from a handy fountain.

As I wiped my mouth, Natalie fluttered up.

"What's the word, mockingbird?" I asked.

"Just a sec-o, Gecko."

I winced.

"Sorry," said Natalie. "Sometimes a girl can't come up with a good rhyme in time."

She filled me in on her spying. It seems Percy and Johnny had gabbed awhile like old friends, then the rattler had slipped something to the raccoon.

"What was it?" I asked.

Natalie shook her head. "I couldn't see. Did you find Luz?"

"Nope. Looks like the squirrel has gone to ground."

"Or to tree," said Natalie.

"Huh?"

She waved a wing at the trees by the playground. "Why don't I fly around and see if I can spot her from above?"

"Want a passenger?" I asked.

"Nothing doing," she said. "This is a solo job."

"Fair enough." I pushed back my hat. "But what can I do?"

Natalie winked. "Doesn't Mr. Mauler have a desk somewhere?"

"Yeah, I think so, in that room where they store the—" I caught her meaning and grinned. "But what kind of low-down character would break into a room and search a teacher's desk?"

Natalie gave me a look. "What kind, indeed?"

While she flew the friendly skies, I hustled over to the storage room where the musical instruments were kept. Recess was slipping away like a cheetah on ice skates. We needed to nail down a suspect, and fast.

Mauler was our best bet.

I tried the door. Locked. I looked up.

One of the high windows was ajar.

Glancing both ways, I scrambled up the wall. With a push and a *creeeeak*, the window swung inward. I poked my head into the darkened room.

Mr. Mauler's desk lay below and to the right. Bingo!

I wedged my body through the narrow opening, getting stuck only once. (So sue me—I'm a gecko who likes his moth milk shakes.) Minus a button, I climbed down the wall on the other side.

All manner of instruments and stacks of sheet music packed the floor. Making for the desk, I eased past a row of horns and drums.

Footsteps scuffed in the hall outside.

I whirled to look.

Boom! My tail whapped the bass drum.

I froze.

Faint voices came from the door. "What was that?" said the higher one.

"Cockroaches," growled the lower voice— Gustav Mauler. "I vill see you later."

A key scratched in the lock. The doorknob rattled.

Frantic, I scanned the room. No cabinets to hide in. No curtains to cover me.

I leaped over the bass drum and ducked behind it.

The door swung open.

Plink! The lights came on.

Holding perfectly still, I watched through the drumskins. A shadowy shape slid past. Moments later, the chair squeaked and a drawer clattered open.

Was Mr. Mauler adding to his stolen booty?

Moving slower than a baby turtle at bedtime, I peeked around the drum.

The big lynx was gazing into his desk with a smile. If only I could see his stash, we could wrap this case up right now.

I leaned out a bit farther...

His yellow eyes lasered into me. "Aha!" he cried. "Ve haff caught ourselves de sneak thief!"

12

Rose Encounters of the Third Kind

Gustav Mauler had played me like a Stradi-whatchamacallit—one of those fancy violins. He hauled me up to Principal Zero's office. On the way, we passed scores of kids returning from recess.

"Dis is de thief!" Mr. Mauler told them.

No big deal. Sticks and stones may break my bones, and all that. I knew Mr. Zero would be calm and understanding.

"You *what*?!" the principal snarled when we stood before him.

"I can explain," I said.

"No need for dot," said Mr. Mauler. "I caught dis lizard in de act."

"You broke into his room?" Mr. Zero asked me, tail lashing.

"Well, technically, yes," I said, "but—"

The principal's gaze shifted to Gustav Mauler. "And what was he stealing?"

"Everything, probably," said the lynx. "You can tell from his beady eyes."

I opened my arms wide. "Search me," I said. "I didn't even take a harmonica."

Mr. Mauler waved a clawed finger in my face. "But only because I caught you."

"*He's* the thief!" I told Principal Zero. "He ripped off my sister!"

"Ridiculous!" the lynx growled. "Don't listen to dis little clown."

My gut clenched like a clammy fist. *"Clowns?"* I gulped, looking around. "Where?"

The principal held up a paw. "Enough." His voice cut through our chatter like a buzz saw through a paper doll. He pointed at me. "Gecko, speak."

"He's been sneaking in and out of empty classrooms," I said.

"Mauler, is this true?" said Mr. Zero.

The lynx shook his shaggy head. "Dis is my job," he blustered. "I go from room to room. De gecko is lying."

Heat rose to my face. "Mama Gecko didn't raise no liars."

"No," said Mr. Zero, "just a kid who doesn't know grammar."

I gestured at the music teacher. "If you check his desk, I bet you'll find the missing items."

Principal Zero pricked up his ears. He stared at Mr. Mauler.

"Oh, no, no," said the lynx, puffing out his chest. "I von't just stand by vhile you search my personal desk on de vord of a mere *student*."

"Oh, really?" said Principal Zero. "Would you prefer to sit instead?"

Despite his threat to "report dis to de teachers' union," Mr. Mauler returned to his office with us. "Dis is absurd," he said as Mr. Zero approached the desk. "I vill tell de superintendent."

The principal sat down in the desk chair. It grumbled like a grandma whose soup is too cold.

I crowded close. "You'll see. It's packed with stolen—"

Mr. Zero slid open the center drawer. It held the usual pencils, paper, and erasers, plus a dozen...

"Plastic roses?" I said.

"See? I told you," said Gustav Mauler, crossing his arms.

Principal Zero narrowed his eyes. "Gecko?"

"That's just a cover-up," I said. "Check the other drawers."

"No!" said Mr. Mauler.

The principal opened a side drawer. This one

contained a woman's scarf, diamond earrings, and Miss Flemm's tiara.

"See? I told you," I said.

Mr. Zero eyed the music teacher, who had turned squirmier than a cupful of earthworms on a full-moon night. "Well?" said the principal. "Care to explain?"

"Dugenzaluff," the lynx muttered, shifting from foot to foot.

"How's that?" asked Mr. Zero.

Mr. Mauler cleared his throat. "Uh, tokens of, er, love," he said at last.

"Love?" I said. "You call *stealing* love?"

The music teacher hung his head. "I have big crushes on several lady teachers," he said. "I—I admit, I sneaked into de rooms and left a rose..."

"And?" said Principal Zero.

"And I took from dem a little token, something to remind me of deir beauty."

Eew. Gross.

I lifted my chin. "So why did you take the computers and pearls and watch? Did you have crushes on their owners, too?"

Mr. Mauler frowned. "Computers? Vatch? Pearls? I did not take dese."

I pawed through his desk, but couldn't find any other missing items. "But you confessed," I said. "You're *guilty*."

"*Ja,*" said Gustav Mauler. "Guilty of love in de first degree." He put out his wrists together. "Lock me up and throw away de key."

Mr. Zero rose and took the music teacher by the shoulder. "This isn't a soap opera, it's a school. And I think your union will want to hear all about your . . . shenanigans."

He led the subdued lynx from the room. I followed. Mr. Zero gave me a look that was as hard to read as test answers on a sweaty palm. (Not that I'd know anything about *that*.)

"Your job's not over, Gecko," said the big cat. "Back to class."

As I watched them leg it down the hall, I stood, flat-footed. My brain spun like a spider in a blender. So there were *two* thieves, not one.

And if Gustav Mauler hadn't swiped my mom's pearls and the other goods, who had?

13

The Tree Stooges

After school, Natalie and I regrouped. As happy kids headed home, gabbing about tomorrow's fair, we sat by the flagpole and swapped stories. Fortunately, hers had a happier ending.

"I found Luz Lipps hiding in a pine at the edge of the playground," she said.

"Sneaky squirrel."

Natalie nodded. "But not sneaky enough. When she left, I trailed her to a big oak tree just off school property. She bent down to its roots..."

"And?"

She shrugged. "The school bell rang, and I had to get back to class."

I shook my head. "What kind of detective are you?"

"The kind that gets good grades," she said. "You should try it sometime."

"What, and give Mr. Zero a heart attack?" I rose. "Come on, partner."

"Where are we going?" asked Natalie.

"Straight to the root of the crime."

Five minutes later, we found ourselves at the foot of a huge, gnarled oak tree. Its twisted limbs cast a dark shade that was heavier than a cheater's conscience.

A creepy feeling brushed across my shoulders, almost as if we were being watched. I searched the branches. "This is it?" I asked.

"Yup," said Natalie, pointing a wing feather. "She was standing right there."

I crunched across the fallen leaves and squatted. Nothing but twigs and beetles. I shot out my tongue and slurped up one of the hard-shelled bugs.

Mmm. After-school snack.

I rapped on the trunk. "Solid as an oak," I said. "No hidden compartments."

Natalie craned her neck and surveyed the branches. "Nothing up there."

Together we circled the great tree, looking high and low. No luck. We came up as empty as a fishcake plate at the end of a piranha's birthday party.

I scratched my head. "There's got to be *something*," I said. "Why did that squirrel come here?"

"To hunt for acorns?" said Natalie with a grin.

"Aw, nuts," I said.

As we left, I still couldn't shake that feeling of being observed. Twice I whirled to catch the watcher, but the scene remained as empty as a beach in a blizzard.

With nothing else to do, I did the unthinkable. I went home and started Ms. Dwyer's double helping of homework.

The afternoon passed in groans and gnashings of teeth. This Dwyer dame was seriously cramping my style. To top it off, I had about as much luck with the homework as I was having with my case.

All through dinner, Pinky shot pleading glances at me. *What about the necklace?* was the question I read in her eyes.

Each time, I lifted my shoulder in a shrug.

I was mopping up the mashed mantis balls in gravy when Mom dropped the bomb.

"Kids," she said, "I was going through my jewelry box today."

Ulp.

"Really?" I said with a poker face.

Pinky's eyes grew as big as soup bowls.

Mom chewed her food. "I wanted to wear something nice for tomorrow night's party, but I couldn't

find my pearls." She peered over her glasses at Pinky and me. "Have either of you seen them?"

Pinky bit her lip. Her chin trembled.

I don't know what possessed me then.

"Uh, yeah," I said. "I was playing, and I got, uh, ink on 'em. So I took the pearls in to have them cleaned."

(Yeah, I realize I said earlier that Mama Gecko didn't raise no liars. So sue me.)

While Mom's lecture broke over me like Hurricane Mary on a toy boat, my sister gazed at me like I was the guy who invented chocolate. At last the tongue-lashing stopped. I promised to return the necklace by the next night, and we cleared the dishes.

Pinky sidled up to me in the kitchen. "Thank you, Chet. Thank you *this* much." She spread her arms as wide as they would go.

I looked down at her. "If you try to hug me with those," I said, "you are *so* dead, sister."

"You're the best, big brother."

I watched her go. Even my death threats weren't scary anymore. With less than twenty-four hours to find the pearls and solve the investigation, I hoped I wasn't losing my touch.

Because if I was, my tail would get much more than just a touch from Mom and Mr. Zero.

14

Every Which Way But Luz

The next day passed in fast motion, like a grass-hopper on a hot griddle. Lessons whipped by in a blur. (Of course, they were a little blurry even when I *wasn't* up against the wall on a big case.)

Ms. Dwyer's scolding over my lame homework seemed to last only a few painful seconds.

I blinked, and it was lunchtime. I blinked again, and it was late recess.

Part of the playground had been blocked off. Workers were setting up the booths and rides. The fair would start in just a few hours, and I had no idea who the real thief was.

Still, Natalie and I kept on plugging. We nosed around for shady serpents, but Percy the rattlesnake was a no-show. We hunted for Luz, but she was tougher to find than the softer side of a sixth-grade bully.

We even trailed Johnny Ringo. But that only earned us another vigorous chase from his pet goon.

Time was running out.

Finally, just before the end of second recess, our persistence paid off. Down the hall that led to the portable classrooms, we spotted that runaway squirrel, Luz Lipps.

I pulled Natalie back. "You keep her busy," I said.

"What are you going to do?" she asked.

"Slip around and cut off her escape."

As I reversed direction, Natalie advanced on Luz, saying, "Are you the hall monitor?"

"Well, I ain't Turkey Lurkey," said the squirrel. The rest of her comment was lost as I circled the building.

Stepping on the gas, I raced down the far side and rounded the corner. Up ahead, Natalie was holding the hall monitor's attention. Luz had her back to me.

I pussyfooted closer.

"But like, I *really* want to know," Natalie was saying in a voice like Malibu Barbie Repeats Third Grade. "Does a hall monitor also monitor the lawns *next to* the halls? And what about the corridors—do you guys do corridors, too?"

The flying squirrel held up her hands. "Cut the chatter!" she said. "I don't give two toots about your newspaper article. I gotta get back to work." And Luz pivoted on her heel—right into my hands.

"Gotcha!" I said, grabbing her shoulders and shoving her up against the wall. "You've been a very naughty squirrel, and now you're gonna sing."

She frowned. "But I don't like music."

I squeezed harder. "Not sing, *sing*," I said. "You know—squeal, spill the beans, blow the whistle?"

Luz looked over at Natalie. "What language is he speaking?"

"Beats me," said Natalie. "But you'd better answer."

I shook the squirrel like a bad habit. "Things have been disappearing from this school, and you're in it up to your fuzzy neck. Start talking."

"Or what?" asked Luz, popping her gum. "You'll beat me up?"

"Huh?" I said. This wasn't working the way I'd expected.

"No matter what," said the squirrel, "you can't do anything worse to me than *he* can."

Natalie and I exchanged a glance. "*He* who?" I asked.

"He who laughs last thinks slowest?" said Natalie.

Luz just kept on chewing.

I rattled her until her gum flew through the air. "Tell us!"

The squirrel's eyes went wide. But her mouth stayed zipped. She kept her trap shut all the way up to Principal Zero's office.

He eyed Luz. "What is this?" said Mr. Zero. "Hall monitor business?"

"She's in on the caper," I said, "but she won't talk. We thought you might..."

The big cat raised an eyebrow. "Fire up the spanking machine?"

Luz turned an interesting shade of beige. Her tail drooped.

"That's the ticket," I said.

Principal Zero snorted. "Strange as it may seem, we have rules to follow. Without proof that she's done something wrong, my paws are tied."

"But she—" said Natalie.

"I'll hold her here through recess," said the cat. "But until a certain numskull PI brings me something solid"—here he glared at me—"that's all I can do. Last chance, Gecko."

Luz Lipps gave us a scornful smile.

My tail curled in frustration. I stomped outside.

"Well, so much for solving this case before the fair," said Natalie as we trudged back to class.

"*Hmph!*" I grumbled.

"You know what this means," she said.

"What?"

Natalie slapped her knee with a wing. "We're a-goin' to the hoedown, podnuh! Yee-hawww!"

I shook my head. "Git along, little birdie, git along."

15

Hoedown and Dirty

I grumped my way through the last couple of lessons. Not even the news that this was Ms. Dwyer's last day could lift my mood.

If I didn't catch the thief by the time the fair started, I would be in deep, deep doo-doo. And so far, I hadn't found the shovel big enough to dig me out.

I was so distracted that I didn't see Shirley's sneak attack coming.

"Oh, Chet?" she said, as we were leaving class.

"Hmm?"

She batted her big green peepers. "Are you, uh, headed to the hoedown after all?"

"Hoedown?" I said, thinking of the case. "Uh, yeah."

Shirley's smile would've blinded a sunbird. "Thanks for being my date. See you at the dance!" And she twirled off to giggle with Bitty Chu.

"Wait!" I said. "What?"

But it was too late. Her cootie ambush had been sprung.

I met Natalie at the edge of the playground. She looked like a country-western song sounds—full of twang and heartbreak and bad fashion choices. My partner sported a huge cowboy hat, red kerchief, and a piece of hay in her beak.

"Howdy, pilgrim!" she said, in a fair imitation of John Wayne.

"What happened here?" I said. "An accident in a farmer factory?"

Natalie tipped her hat. "Just showin' some school spirit, stranger. Hey, that reminds me: Knock, knock."

"Natalie, we don't have time for this now."

"Knock, knock." She stared at me.

"Oh, all right," I said. "Who's there?"

"Amarillo."

I sighed. "Amarillo who?"

"Amarillo-fashioned cowboy!" She cackled. "Get it? *Real old-fashioned?*"

"I get it. Now can we get out of here?"

Natalie tossed her hay aside. "Let's mosey, podnuh."

By this time, the school was filling up with kids and parents, many of whom were dressed like Natalie. I winced. Private eyes and cowpokes don't mix.

The playground had a strange Wild-Bill-Hickok-Meets-Barnum-and-Bailey feel. Hay bales and corrals stood cheek by jowl with the Tilt-A-Whirl and Whack-A-Worm booths. Jugglers and stilt walkers competed with lasso twirlers and pony wranglers. And over by the trees, a huge circus tent held (according to its banner) the Wonders of the Western World.

Two off-duty policemen in cowboy duds stood by its door. They were about as inconspicuous as a scorpion on a shortcake. (But not nearly as tasty.)

I nudged Natalie. "See the cops?"

"How can you tell?" she asked.

"Real cowboys don't carry billy clubs and walkie-talkies."

She fluffed her feathers. "You get the feeling Mr. Zero is worried about the thief striking again? Maybe going after the Flubberjee Egg?"

"Just a little, yeah."

It was encouraging to know how much faith our principal had in us.

Natalie and I walked the circuit, keeping an eye peeled for Luz Lipps, Percy the rattlesnake, and any other suspicious characters.

"Notice anything?" said Natalie.

"You're not the only one dressed like Hopalong McHayseed?"

"Nope," she said. "No clowns."

I breathed a silent sigh of relief.

As we passed the kissing booth, a mouse named Frenchy LaTrine called out.

"Hey, Chet!" she said, toying with her ribbon. "Want to buy a smooch?"

I stepped back. "*Eew.* You couldn't *pay* me to pucker up."

"It's for a good cause." She batted her fudge brown eyes at me.

"I've got a better one," I said. "Avoiding your cooties."

Natalie snickered. We rounded a group of kids, and I bumped right into Johnny Ringo.

"Excuse you, you didn't see me," I said.

"Watch it, buster," growled the sleek raccoon.

Rolf the wolverine stood behind him, flexing his muscles. "You like I should bimp 'em, boss?"

Ringo straightened his vest. "Nah, we'll settle their hash later."

"What are *you* up to?" said Natalie.

"It's a free country," said the raccoon. "I'm just being me."

I eyed him and his pet wolverine. "That's what I'm afraid of."

"I got my ticket, amigo," Johnny said, smiling. "I'm gonna go see the wonders just like everyone else. And there's nothing you can do to stop me."

I hate it when the bad guys are right.

Satisfying myself with a parting sneer, I turned to go. Just then, wild fiddle music burst from speakers mounted on poles. Although it sounded to me like the death throes of a bobcat with laryngitis, the crowd seemed excited.

Coach Stroganoff's voice boomed through the speakers. "Come on over to the Hens' Hoedown, cowpokes! It's chickies' choice; time to shake your tail feathers!"

Natalie looked over at me. "*Chickies'* choice? Coach needs some lessons in how to talk about girls."

"That's not all he needs," I said. "Never mind, we've got bigger bugs to fry."

But before I could take ten steps, someone grabbed my tail.

"Easy on the merchandise," I said. "That thing comes off."

"Where are you going?" said Shirley Chameleon. "We have a dance date, remember?"

I turned and reclaimed my tail. "I must have been dreaming," I said. "Or insane."

"But you *promised*," said Shirley with a pout.

Natalie leaned over my shoulder. "A promise is a promise, big guy."

"But—" I said.

"Go dance with your girlfriend," said Natalie. "I'll keep on patrolling."

"That's super!" said Shirley, seizing my arm.

"She's *not* my girlfriend," I protested as the chameleon dragged me off.

The dance floor was a big square surrounded by hay bales, over near the Wonders of the Western World tent. Chattering girls linked arms with boys who looked as nervous as garden slugs in a salt mine.

Bo Newt was so discombobulated, he tripped over his own tail and sprawled in the dirt. Onlookers clapped and cheered.

Coach Stroganoff, a massive groundhog in a dinky yellow hat, stood on a bale. He bellowed out the dance instructions:

> *"Alley-oop left with your left hand,*
> *Do-si-do with a baby grand,*
> *Promenade and hinkey-doo,*
> *Squeeze your partner, coochie-coo!"*

He might just as well have been reciting the times tables in ancient Greek, but a few couples actually made the same moves. Shirley tugged me into their midst.

"Isn't this *fun*?" she gushed.

"As jolly as a day at the dentist's office." I tried not to stub my toes.

As we whirled about, I spotted Johnny Ringo's mocking face in the crowd. When I looked again, it had vanished.

The second song started. Shirley grabbed my hands.

I said a silent prayer: *Please get me off this dance floor. Any distraction will do.*

Five seconds later, my prayer was answered. And I realized I should have been more specific.

Honking madly, a small pink car squealed to a halt. The doors burst open, and a pack of characters popped out. Deranged characters with wild hair, painted faces, and red, rubbery noses.

No, not tax accountants.

Clowns.

16

Bad, Bad Leroy Clown

The onlookers cheered as a seemingly impossible number of clowns piled out of the pint-sized car. Even the cops at the tent ambled forward to see.

The jokers juggled eggs and footballs and firecrackers; they slipped on banana peels. They honked their shiny horns and wove in and out of the crowd, leering with their crazy clown faces and laughing their creepy clown laughs.

My palms got clammier than the New England seashore. My stomach clenched. "Urgh," I moaned, backing away.

"What's the matter?" asked Shirley.

"Hate . . . clowns," I said through clenched teeth. "Must . . . go."

"Chet?"

And I staggered away from their puke pink car and spooky, rubber-kneed antics. Pushing through the crowd, I stumbled blindly on.

Cool, dark shade fell over me, and I stopped. Blinking, I looked around my sanctuary: the big tent.

It was deserted. Everyone had left to see the painted weirdos, who were now shooting off fireworks.

I sagged against a tent pole and caught my breath. After a minute, I walked around stiff-legged, shaking it off.

Here were models of the pyramids, gleaming golden in the subdued light. There stood a big Aztec-looking stone disk, covered with carvings.

I wasn't sure what this odd mishmash had to do with a school fair, but it looked pretty cool. Toddling onward, I noticed a spangled cowboy hat, a life-size sculpture of an emerald cow, and copies of the *Mona Lisa* and other fancy-pants paintings.

And then, at the far end of the tent, I saw it: on a pedestal by itself, the Flubberjee Egg.

Wow.

Lit by a single spotlight, cradled on black velvet, the egg was bigger than my head and encrusted with enough rubies and sapphires to make an empress drool. It pulled me closer and closer.

Then a thought struck me: Why was it un-protected?

A flicker of movement caught my eye. I looked up. There was the glass case, hanging safely in the coils of...a really, *really* big snake.

I gasped.

"Yesss," he hissed. "Beautiful, isssn't it?"

"Uh, yeah."

The giant boa had scaled the tent's steel frame. His massive body was as thick as a tuba and twice as twisty. His gaze was as cold as a polar bear's heinie.

The snake effortlessly held the glass case with his tail while his front half slithered down to just above my head.

I stepped back.

"Balthazar Boa, at your ssservice," he said. His forked tongue flitted out, and his red eyes gleamed.

I clenched my fists. "So *you're* the scumbag that ripped off my little sister."

"Why, yesss."

"You robbed the wrong student, buster."

A nasty grin played across his mug. "Ooh. Bold wordsss from the cluelesss shamusss. How droll."

I hate it when the bad guys mock.

"Oh, yeah?" I said. "We already caught your partner in crime, Luz Lipps."

The boa slithered a little lower. "Have you? I bet she didn't confesss."

"Not yet," said Natalie from behind me. "But she will."

I shot her a warm glance. "That's right. We detectives have our ways."

Balthazar Boa chuckled, a sound like dead leaves blowing over a gravestone. "Your waysss? Like the way you misssed me at the serpentsss' protesst?"

"You were the anaconda with the signs?" I said, shaking my head. "Dang. I always did have a problem telling boy snakes from girl snakes."

Natalie crossed the tent floor. "So you and Percy are in it together."

The boa scoffed. "That wusss? Percy and his idealisstic foolsss provided a perfect cover for me to cassse the ssschool and contact my little thievesss."

Natalie cocked her head. "But why did Luz leave school grounds that day?"

Bal Boa slithered closer still. We backed up.

"To make a drop-off at my tree, of courssse," he said.

"Your tree?" Natalie elbowed me. "I *told* you we were being watched."

"No, you didn't," I said. "*I* told you."

The huge snake scowled. "Enough chitchat. I'm

taking thisss egg, and you can't do a thing to ssstop me."

"Oh, yeah?" I circled nearer to the treasure. "And how will you carry it without any hands, Stretch?"

I reached for the jeweled egg.

"Like thisss," said the boa. *Wham-bam!* His wedge-shaped head shot out, and the Flubberjee Egg was gone!

"Put that back!" cried Natalie.

"Unh-hrmm," said Bal Boa around the egg in his mouth.

"Natalie, get the cops!" I cried.

She crouched, ready for action. "What are you going to do?"

I eyeballed the snake, now slithering back up onto the tent frame. "I'll, uh, think of something. Go!"

She flew to the door.

Just then—*kzzatch!*—the glass case shattered on the floor, and—*ka-ka-BOOOM!*—the fireworks exploded outside.

"You'll never get away," I said. "You can't slither fast enough."

"Hghah!" laughed Balthazar Boa. The egg had worked its way into his throat. "I don't hghave to!"

Footsteps pounded behind me. I whirled. Was it the cops?

No such luck. Two beefy iguanas stood there, dressed in whiteface, baggy pants, and multicolored wigs.

"Gah," I said, staggering back.

Not clowns again.

Anything but clowns.

17

Egg, Borrow, and Steal

The painted iguanas stood between me and the door. Somehow, under the makeup, they seemed familiar.

"You don't listen too good, do you, bright boy?" said Squinchy Eye. "We told you to leave town."

Nose Ring advanced on me. Under his ruff, he wore pearls—Mom's pearls.

"Give...those...back," I choked out.

But I couldn't raise a finger. I crouched against the wall, cornered by clowns.

"Can oy squeeze 'im now?" said Nose Ring.

"Don't sssqueeze *hghim,*" said the massive boa. "Sssqueeze *me.*"

Thunk! He plummeted to the floor like an elephant high-wire act.

"Ooh," said Nose Ring. "Eight-point-five!"

Squinchy Eye addressed the snake. "I don't follow, chief."

"Danged peristalsisss," said Boa, slithering up to them. "I cgh-can't stop sssswallowing the egg, so you must sssqueeze it ogh-out of me."

"Ah, right you are," said the iguana. "Grab his tail," he told Nose Ring.

The second lizard moved into place. Squinchy Eye wrapped his hands around the bulge in the snake's gullet.

"Hghurry," said Balthazar Boa. "The copsss..."

Squinchy Eye grinned. "They're busy putting out the fire."

"W-what fire?" I asked, still unsteady.

"The one we started with fireworks, of course." He gave a yank on the egg.

"Cgh-careful," choked the boa.

Paralyzed by Bozo-phobia, my mind was as gummed up as the bottom of a balcony seat at the movies. Should I run for help? Should I try to fight the goons? Or should I just curl into a ball and hide?

I hugged my arms and fought for control. The clowns seemed huge and hideous, bulging with jolly menace. I bit my lip and forced myself to look at them without bawling like a baby.

The iguanas were stretching the boa like a

fourteen-foot rubber band. Nose Ring dug in his heels and pulled the tail for all he was worth, while his partner kept tugging at the bulge.

Soon they'd have the egg.

For my sister, for my school, I had to stop them. Painfully, with all my limbs shaking, I stood up straight.

"Hgh! Khaugh!" choked Bal Boa, eyes popping.

Squinchy Eye worked the egg closer and closer to the snake's mouth. And then, just behind the jaws, it stuck fast.

"Pull!" cried Nose Ring.

Knees knocking louder than a pushy door-to-door salesman, I took a step toward them.

"I'm pulling," said Squinchy Eye.

"Phugh hghagha!" choked the snake.

"Oy fink 'e said, *Pull 'arder,*" said Nose Ring.

Sweat popped on my forehead. I managed another step, and another.

Squinchy Eye took a fresh grip and braced himself. "All right, mate, big jerk on three. One . . . two . . . three!"

The iguanas leaned in opposite directions, and—*thoom!*—the Flubberjee Egg flew from the boa's jaws, bounced off Squinchy Eye's forehead, and sailed straight toward me.

Though my brain still felt frozen, instinct took

over. My tongue zipped out, wrapped around the egg, and reeled it in.

Unfortunately, I hadn't realized how heavy it was.

Whump!

The Flubberjee Egg hit the floor, bruising my poor tongue in the process.

Pain is a good waker-upper. I reeled in my stinger, jumped forward, and snatched up the treasure in my arms.

"Get it!" cried the boa.

The iguanas closed in. I dodged and ducked under their grabs.

"Block the door!" grunted Squinchy Eye to his fellow clown. Nose Ring trotted back to the entrance.

I tried to squeeze out under the tent wall, but it was nailed down. Squinchy Eye snatched at me again. I spun away.

The boa was scaling the tent frame, cutting off another getaway route. (Not that I could climb the walls with the bulky egg in my arms.)

How could I escape?

"It's no use, Gecko," said Squinchy Eye. "Cry uncle!"

I raced through the tent, darting between the displays. Squinchy Eye popped up behind the pyramids and sent me doubling back, and then—

Floomp! The sky fell on me.

I hit the floor, with the treasure beneath me.

The great weight pinning me down turned out to be the back half of Balthazar Boa, which was quickly encircling my legs.

"Hey!" I cried, kicking.

No use. The coils wound higher.

I lurched upright, arms clutching the Flubberjee Egg.

The boa's face dropped in front of me. "Give it," he said. "It'sss mine."

"Never!" I blustered.

Things were starting to look as bleak as a week without water in the Kalahari Desert. Just then, the tent door opened, letting in a blast of afternoon sunlight.

The iguanas froze.

Was it the cops?

"*There* you are!" cried Shirley Chameleon.

"Shirley, help!" I said. "We can't let him get the—"

"I was so worried," she said. Emotions chased across her face like the monkey after the weasel. "And here I thought you were sick."

"I was, but then I—"

Shirley's eyes blazed. She brushed Nose Ring aside and stalked toward me. "Of all the rude, inconsiderate, two-faced—"

"Huh?"

"You agree to be my date, and then you *disappear*? I don't think so!" Shirley stood before me, hands on hips.

"But I was trying to, *ugh*," I said as the snake squeezed my belly.

"I don't care!" yelled Shirley. "I'm so mad at you. See if I ever speak to you again!" She turned away.

"Wait!" I cried, struggling to catch a breath. "Call, *ugh*, Mr. Zero. Tell him the, *ugh*, thief is—"

"Typical!" said Shirley. "Always wrapped up in your stupid detective games, and no time for relationships."

"But—" I gasped.

She flounced toward the exit. "You can do your own errands, Mr. PI Gecko. I wash my hands of you!"

The door closed behind her.

"Now where were we?" said Balthazar Boa. "Oh, yesss. You were about to give me the egg."

His coils tightened even more, crushing all the air from my chest.

My sides ached. My head began to pound like King Kong playing a jungle drum solo. *Must breathe,* said my lungs, but I had no answer for them.

"Take it from him," said the snake.

Through my dimming vision, the iguana clowns

sauntered forward. They took the Flubberjee Egg, easy as slurping mosquito larva from a barrel.

"Ugh!" I choked out.

The world was growing darker, darker. Then, in the midst of the darkness, a light!

Was I passing over to the Other Side?

Was this the end of Chet Gecko?

18

Fair and Square

"**D**rop that lizard!" a voice growled.

Apparently the spirits on the Other Side sounded just like Big Fat Zero.

I squinted into the light.

The principal stood in the doorway, flanked by two cops and a mockingbird. "Do it now!" he snapped.

The coils relaxed. I sagged to my knees.

Air rushed into my lungs like preschoolers into a pool party. I sucked in one breath, then another. Oxygen had never tasted so good—better than a triple-decker centipede brownie cake with banana-slug icing.

"Took you . . . long enough," I rasped.

Natalie rushed to my side. "Easy, partner."

"Nice delaying action, Gecko," said Principal Zero, padding forward.

"Had him right . . . where I wanted him," I said.

The cops took the jeweled egg from Squinchy Eye and Nose Ring, and then slapped the handcuffs on them.

But they'd forgotten about one crook.

"You'll never catch me, coppersss!" Balthazar Boa snarled. He slithered for the tent pole and began to climb.

Bzzzzkt!

Thump!

An electric shock from a flatfoot's stun gun dropped the big snake back to earth.

While the cops rolled the boa up like a fire hose and bound him with duct tape, Principal Zero grilled the iguanas. They sang like a boy band—a boy band full of ugly criminals made up to look like Bozo.

Turns out, Balthazar Boa had put together a slick little theft ring at Emerson Hicky. A half-dozen sixth-grade thieves lifted the loot, which they then passed to Luz by smooching. Since she could go anywhere unchallenged, the hall monitor carried the goods in her puffy cheeks all the way to the boa's tree.

"What about the computers?" said Mr. Zero.

"They was too 'eavy," said Nose Ring. "So we nicked 'em at night."

Something was bugging me. "But how did you get into the classrooms in the first place?" I asked.

"The janitor," said Squinchy Eye.

Natalie gasped. "Not Maureen DeBree!"

"Nah," said Nose Ring. "The rabbit."

"She unlocked the classrooms; we gave her some dough for her family," said Squinchy Eye. He shook his head. "Shoot. And it was such a sweet setup."

"Tell it to the judge," said Principal Zero.

The cops started to lead the deflated-looking iguanas away.

"Wait," I said, walking up to Nose Ring. "Those pearls don't match your outfit." I unclasped the necklace and pocketed it.

He sulked. "That's no way to treat a lady."

The flatfoots marched their captives out, rolling the coiled snake between them like a floppy wheel.

Outside the tent, the fair was still in full swing. Kids munched cotton-candy dragonflies, played ring-toss, dunked teachers, and gabbed with friends. They had no clue what had gone down inside the big tent.

A detective's job is a thankless one.

Principal Zero clapped his paws onto Natalie's and my shoulders. "Good work, private eyes. You deserve a reward."

Well, maybe not *entirely* thankless.

"That's not necessary, sir," said Natalie.

I elbowed her. "Now, now. Don't insult our principal."

The huge cat steered us over to the refreshment booth and plunked a bill onto the counter. My eyes grew big at the sight of cotton candy, butterscotch sweat bees, horsefly pie, and candied apple worms.

"How about a firm handshake and a warm soda?" said Mr. Zero.

He shook hands with each of us and bought us drinks.

"Uh, how about that free pass for the next three times I get in trouble?" I asked.

The cat smoothed his chin fur. "Let's see . . . you didn't catch the thief on time, I had to pay for extra security from my own pocket, and you almost lost the egg," he said. "Gecko, you're lucky to get a soda."

That's our principal. All heart.

Natalie and I strolled through the fair, sipping our drinks. After what I'd been through, even the screeching fiddles of the hoedown seemed like a lullaby.

As we passed the dance floor, Shirley Chameleon was *do-si-do*ing around Bo Newt. When she saw me, she stuck out her tongue and blew a loud raspberry.

"Haven't lost your touch with the ladies, I see," said Natalie.

"She says she never wants to speak to me again."

Natalie rested a wing tip on my arm. "Chet, I'm sorry to hear that."

"Sorry?" I said. "At least I got *some* kind of reward from this screwy case."

Across the way, I spotted my sister walking with my mom. "There's Pinky. She's been pretty worried. I should go over and break the good news."

"So you can have a tender brother-sister moment when you tell her how you got her out of trouble?" Natalie beamed.

I rolled my eyes. "Are you kidding? She owes me big-time, and I'm ready to start collecting."

Just then, Pinky spotted me. When she made with the anxious eyes, I gave her a discreet thumbs-up. My sister's smile lit up the fair.

I smiled back. After all, she may be a brat, but she's my brat.

Before I could join Pinky, Natalie pointed at the dunking booth. "Hey, isn't that your substitute teacher on the hot seat?"

I looked. Sure enough, a surly porcupine sat on her perch above the pool.

"Want to have a try after you talk to Pinky?" asked Natalie.

"Before," I said, crossing to the booth.

"But I thought family came first," she said.

I plunked four quarters down onto the counter. "Family reunions are sweet, my friend. But revenge is even sweeter."

"Aw, Chet, you don't mean that."

"Don't I?" I arched an eyebrow. "Just watch me, partner."

And I picked up the first softball.

Look for more mysteries from the Tattered Casebook of Chet Gecko in hardcover and paperback

Case #1 *The Chameleon Wore Chartreuse*

Some cases start rough, some cases start easy. This one started with a dame. (That's what we private eyes call a girl.) She was cute and green and scaly. She looked like trouble and smelled like . . . grasshoppers.

Shirley Chameleon came to me when her little brother, Billy, turned up missing. (I suspect she also came to spread cooties, but that's another story.) She turned on the tears. She promised me some stinkbug pie. I said I'd find the brat.

But when his trail led to a certain stinky-breathed, bad-tempered, jumbo-sized Gila monster, I thought I'd bitten off more than I could chew. Worse, I had to chew fast: If I didn't find Billy in time, it would be bye-bye, stinkbug pie.

Case #2 *The Mystery of Mr. Nice*

How would you know if some criminal mastermind tried to impersonate your principal? My first clue: He was nice to me.

This fiend tried everything—flattery, friendship, food—but he still couldn't keep me off the case. Natalie and I followed a trail of clues as thin as the cheese on a cafeteria hamburger. And we found a ring of corruption that went from the janitor right up to Mr. Big.

In the nick of time, we rescued Principal Zero and busted up the PTA meeting, putting a stop to the evil genius. And what thanks did we get? Just the usual. A cold handshake and a warm soda.

But that's all in a day's work for a private eye.

Case #3   *Farewell, My Lunchbag*

If danger is my business, then dinner is my passion. I'll take any case if the pay is right. And what pay could be better than Mothloaf Surprise?

At least that's what I thought. But in this particular case, I almost paid the ultimate price for good grub.

Cafeteria lady Mrs. Bagoong hired me to track down whoever was stealing her food supplies. The long, slimy trail led too close to my own backyard for comfort.

And much, much too close to the very scary Jimmy "King" Cobra. Without the help of Natalie Attired and our school janitor, Maureen DeBree, I would've been gecko sushi.

Case #4   *The Big Nap*

My grades were lower than a salamander's slippers, and my bank account was trying to crawl under a duck's belly. So why did I take a case that didn't pay anything?

Put it this way: Would *you* stand by and watch some

evil power turn *your* classmates into hypnotized zombies? (If that wasn't just what normally happened to them in math class, I mean.)

My investigations revealed a plot meaner than a roomful of rhinos with diaper rash.

Someone at Emerson Hicky was using a sinister video game to put more and more students into la-la-land. And it was up to me to stop it, pronto—before that someone caught up with me, and I found myself taking the Big Nap.

Case #5   *The Hamster of the Baskervilles*

Elementary school is a wild place. But this was ridiculous.

Someone—or some*thing*—was tearing up Emerson Hicky. Classrooms were trashed. Walls were gnawed. Mysterious tunnels riddled the playground like worm chunks in a pan of earthworm lasagna.

But nobody could spot the culprit, let alone catch him.

I don't believe in the supernatural. My idea of voodoo is my mom's cockroach-ripple ice cream.

Then, a teacher reported seeing a monster on full-moon night, and I got the call.

At the end of a twisted trail of clues, I had to answer the burning question: Was it a vicious, supernatural were-hamster on the loose, or just another Science Fair project gone wrong?

Case #6 *This Gum for Hire*

Never thought I'd see the day when one of my worst enemies would hire me for a case. Herman the Gila Monster was a sixth-grade hoodlum with a first-rate left hook. He told me someone was disappearing the football team, and he had to put a stop to it. *Big whoop.*

He told me he was being blamed for the kidnappings, and he had to clear his name. *Boo hoo.*

Then he said that I could either take the case and earn a nice reward, or have my face rearranged like a bargain-basement Picasso painted by a spastic chimp.

I took the case.

But before I could find the kidnapper, I had to go undercover. And that meant facing something that scared me worse than a chorus line of criminals in steel-toed boots: P.E. class.

Case #7 *The Malted Falcon*

It was tall, dark, and chocolatey—the stuff dreams are made of. It was a treat so titanic that nobody had been able to finish one single-handedly (or even single-mouthedly). It was the Malted Falcon.

How far would you go for the ultimate dessert? Somebody went too far, and that's where I came in.

The local sweets shop held a contest. The prize: a year's supply of free Malted Falcons. Some lucky kid scored the winning ticket. She brought it to school for show-and-tell.

But after she showed it, somebody swiped it. And no one would tell where it went.

Following a strong hunch and an even stronger sweet tooth, I tracked the ticket through a web of lies more tangled than a rattlesnake doing the rumba. But the time to claim the prize was fast approaching. Would the villain get the sweet treat—or his just desserts?

Case #8 *Trouble Is My Beeswax*

Okay, I confess. When test time rolls around, I'm as tempted as the next lizard to let my eyeballs do the walking . . . to my neighbor's paper.

But Mrs. Gecko didn't raise no cheaters. (Some language manglers, perhaps.) So when a routine investigation uncovered a test-cheating ring at Emerson Hicky, I gave myself a new case: Put the cheaters out of business.

Easier said than done. Those double-dealers were slicker than a frog's fanny and twice as slimy.

Oh, and there was one other small problem: All the evidence pointed to two dames. The ringleader was either the glamorous Lacey Vail, or my own classmate Shirley Chameleon.

Sheesh. The only thing I hate worse than an empty Pillbug Crunch wrapper is a case full of dizzy dames.

Case #9 *Give My Regrets to Broadway*

Some things you can't escape, however hard you try—like dentist appointments, visits with strange-smelling relatives, and being in the fourth-grade play. I had always left the acting to my smart-aleck pal, Natalie, but now it was my turn in the spotlight.

Stage fright? Me? You're talking about a gecko who has laughed at danger, chuckled at catastrophe, and sneezed at sinister plots.

I was terrified.

Not because of the acting, mind you. The script called for me to share a major lip-lock with Shirley Chameleon—Cootie Queen of the Universe!

And while I was trying to avoid that trap, a simple missing persons case took a turn for the worse—right into the middle of my play. Would opening night spell curtains for my client? And, more important, would someone invent a cure for cooties? But no matter—whatever happens, the sleuth must go on.

Case #10 *Murder, My Tweet*

Some things at school you can count on. Pop quizzes always pop up just after you've spent your study time studying comics. Chef's Surprise is always a surprise, but never a good one. And no matter how much you learn today, they always make you come back tomorrow.

But sometimes, Emerson Hicky amazes you. And just like finding a killer bee in a box of Earwig Puffs, you're left shocked, stung, and discombobulated.

Foul play struck at my school; that's nothing new.

But then the finger of suspicion pointed straight at my favorite fowl: Natalie Attired. Framed as a blackmailer, my partner was booted out of Emerson Hicky quicker than a hoptoad on a hot plate.

I tackled the case for free. Mess with my partner, mess with me.

Then things took a turn for the worse. Just when I thought I might clear her name, Natalie disappeared. And worse still, she left behind one clue: a reddish smear that looked kinda like the jelly from a beetle-jelly sandwich but raised an ugly question: Was it murder, or something serious?

Case #11 *The Possum Always Rings Twice*

In my time, I've tackled cases stickier than a spider's handshake and harder than three-year-old boll weevil taffy. But nothing compares to the job that landed me knee-deep in school politics.

What seemed like a straightforward case of extortion during Emerson Hicky's student-council election ended up taking more twists and turns than an anaconda's lunch. It became a battle royal for control of the school. (Not that I necessarily believe school is worth fighting for, but a gecko's gotta do *something* with his days.)

In the end, my politicking landed me in one of the tightest spots I've ever encountered. Was I savvy enough to escape with my skin? Let me put it this way: Just like a politician, this is one private eye who always shoots from the lip.

Case #12 *Key Lardo*

Working this case, I nearly lost my detective mojo—and to a guy so dim, he'd probably play goalie for the darts team. True, he was only a cog in a larger conspiracy. But this big buttinsky made my life more uncomfortable than a porcupine's underpants.

Was he a cop? A truant officer? A gorilla with a grudge? Even worse: A rival detective. His name was Bland. *James* Bland. And he was cracking cases faster than a . . . well, *much* faster than I was.

My reputation took a nosedive. And I nearly followed it—straight into the slammer. Fighting back with all my moxie, I bent the rules, blundered into blind alleys, and stepped on more than a few toes.

Was I right? Was I wrong? I'll tell you this: I made my share of mistakes. But I believe that if you can't laugh at yourself . . . make fun of someone else.